To James,
Kno...
...
...

JoAnne.

Dogs
Really Do Go To
Heaven

A 'Tail' To Lift Your Heart

JoAnne Callaway

Foreword by Kat Kerr

Dogs Really Do Go To Heaven
A 'Tail' To Lift Your Heart
by JoAnne Callaway

Cover and all Graphic Art Illustrated by Debra Cloud of
"The Cloud Company"

Printed in the United States of America

ISBN 9781628399974

www.xulonpress.com

Special Thanks

First I would like to thank My Heavenly Father who gave me the 'witty idea' and the grace to write this book despite the trials that ensued during this journey.

I appreciate all the prayers and words of encouragement from my dear friend and prayer partner Miki Zuliani throughout the writing of this book.

Thank you to Kat Kerr for your obedience and love in sharing the original message of heaven with all who are willing to listen and being the inspiration for me to even attempt to write this book. And thank you for taking the time out of your busy schedule to write the foreword. It is so greatly appreciated.

Great thanks to Debra Cloud who, through her own excitement and inspiration from Kat, created incredible graphics and design for the cover of this book and the pictures within. I appreciate all the work that went into these unique creations. Also for all the assistance with formatting and all the other little technicalities you so graciously helped me with!

Thank you to my sister Maureen Leavey for taking the time to help with the final edit and overview of the book.

Thank you to all my relatives and friends who prayed and always had words of encouragement as I was writing this book.

I love you all and appreciate the uniqueness of all your giftings!

Dedication

In the process of writing this book I had two members of my family, my father Charles Callaway (April 28), and my brother Brian (May 3), leave this earth for their eternal home in heaven.

Seven weeks later my beloved dog Chelsea, 9rs. old, departed this life on June 22, 2013.

I dedicate this book to all of them knowing full well that one day, in the not too distant future by heavens standards, we will all be reunited to love one another and live in joy for all of eternity in that heavenly realm we will call HOME.

My Precious Dog

There's not a day that passes by,
Where a little tear falls from my eye.
Remembering you my sweet, sweet pet,
A tender face I can never forget.
Your eyes so bright that used to shine,
Whenever they looked up to mine.
Right now my heart feels ever so low
Because I really miss you so.
But there's a hope within this heart,
Knowing soon we will not be apart.
The promise of our precious Lord,
Assures me of His wondrous love.
I know for sure that I will see,
A day when you will be with me.
And there in heavens glorious home,
We'll be together, no longer alone.

JoAnne

In Memory of My Sweet Chelsea
May 8, 2004 – June 22, 2013

2012/04/01

Your bright little light is now shining in heaven.
You are playing with your friends and waiting for me.

Table of Contents

Foreword. xiii

Preface xv

Introduction. xvii

Chapter One: The Beauty of Heaven 19

Chapter Two: My Life on Earth 21

Chapter Three: Stepping into the Spirit Realm 25

Chapter Four: My New Home 29

Chapter Five: A Whole New World 32

Chapter Six: Meeting New Friends 38

Chapter Seven: New Adventures with Old Friends 42

Chapter Eight: Winter Wonderland 46

Chapter Nine: Roller Coasters and Other Surprises 55

Chapter Ten: More Fun in the Amusement Park 60

Chapter Eleven: I Can See Home From Here 63

Chapter Twelve: The Valley of the Falls. 66

Chapter Thirteen: Fragrance to Fill the Senses 75

Chapter Fourteen: A New Family Member. 81

Chapter Fifteen: Talking to the Trees? 85

Chapter Sixteen: Visiting Mansions on the Crystal Sea 91

Chapter Seventeen: A Real Jungle Experience 100

Chapter Eighteen: Big Waves and Pet Portals. 107

Chapter Nineteen: Mansions in the Sky 111

Chapter Twenty: Is This For Real? 117

Chapter Twenty One: Nothing is Forgotten in Heaven 123

Chapter Twenty Two: Celebrating God's Way 127

Foreword

Heaven is the most Amazing, Captivating 'Life Filled' place I have ever seen because the Father is unlimited in His ability to love us and create for us. He truly gives us the desires of our hearts by consuming us with His presence, allowing us to live near our friends and family and YES, even our beloved pets.

Having gone on tours of Heaven many times, I remember vividly the time He caught me up and showed me a very long line of pets (that had belonged to my siblings and myself) which were following my Dad on his ranch! I laughed as I recognized them; the two little mice that lived in a hole in the wall of the New York flat we had before moving to Florida, Charlie my brothers alligator, Max a duck my other brother had when he was 9, many dogs, cats, birds, lizards, a chicken named Maggie, a huge frog named Spot and a cardinal we had rescued named Bozo and many more!

The Father assured me there was only one reason He brought our pets to Heaven, it was because we LOVED them. He said, "Tell the doubters it is not a subject intended for theological discussion (it has nothing to do with whether they can be 'born again' or not) I simply decided to bless those that Love Me".

JoAnne Callaway, author of this book, 'DOGS REALLY DO GO TO HEAVEN', got a 'witty idea' from the Father to bring HOPE to all those who have experienced the death of their pets by sharing TRUTH about them living in Heaven.

As you go on this exciting tour with Pal, the grief will lift and you will understand the love God has for both you and your pets. You never lose when you give yourself to Jesus Christ; He even gives us the joy of living through eternity with our 'extended' family members, our pets!

Kat Kerr, Author of Revealing Heaven series

Preface

For centuries mankind has been curious about Heaven. Does it even exist? Do we actually go somewhere after we die? Scientists have denied its existence yet millions of dollars are spent searching the universe trying to unlock the mysteries that may possibly give us reason to believe there is such a place. This search may continue for years to come but according to the Bible no one will ever find it because it is a spiritual place, a supernatural place where natural things cannot be found.

This book is based on Biblical truths and experiential knowledge revealed to us through a Prophetic Revelator I came to hear about a few months ago. Kat Kerr, is a woman who God has used in an extraordinary way to bring light, life, and truth to this world by catching her up in the spirit to heaven and revealing to her the wonders of His Glory and Majesty. He has shown her in great detail the reality and truth of heaven's existence.

Kat has been taken on heavenly journeys for the past 16 years, has written two books called 'Revealing Heaven I and II,' and is eventually, as the Lord directs, writing a third book. She now travels internationally bringing the joyful news that the Father has wanted her to release to the world. He (God) has told her that He WANTS His children to know there is a heaven, a home to which we one day, if we are believers, will go, and He wants to reveal to us the reality of what His home is really like. My heart was especially blessed by the fact that He showed her, for certain, that our pets are in heaven too. Kat is bringing this message of hope and love to many and soon the whole world will hear the message she's been given to share.

This book is based on some of the heavenly encounters that Kat has experienced although the activities that the dogs are involved in, is merely my own imagination. It is my hope that you, the reader, will just enjoy the story which is meant to be fun and engaging but realizing all the while that much of it is real.

I have been a dog lover all my life and I know there are millions of people like me out there who would feel devastated if their beloved pets couldn't share eternity with them. It is so encouraging to me that even though there is always sadness when a pet passes on, there is a light at the end of the tunnel when we understand that we will be together again one day. Heaven will indeed be a glorious place!

I would like to thank Kat Kerr for her obedience in laying her own life down in order to bring these heavenly revelations to us. Kat has given everything of herself so that you and I can be blessed beyond measure and know beyond the shadow of a doubt that Heaven really does exist. I highly recommend that you read Kat's books as they are the factual revelations of her encounters in heaven and they will change your life forever. They sure changed mine!

Introduction

I never thought that in the midst writing this book I would be tested again with the loss of another dog. Chelsea was the last of the four dogs I've had since 1983 and was a mere 9 years old; young to me considering all my dogs have lived to see 13 and 14 years. She was a very sweet, lovable dog who went everywhere with me, even to work when I was an activity director at a Retirement Residence for Seniors. She had become the 'resident dog' and everyone just loved her. She was so special to me because she was the last, and she followed me like a shadow which is often what I said I should have named her.

I found, unfortunately too late, that she had a large mass next to her heart, which had probably been there for a while. By the time any symptoms had shown up, she developed severe respiratory distress and it was too late to help her. I was forced to have her euthanized. I will miss her very much but I know that she is now in a much better place watching and waiting for me to one day be reunited with her and all of my other pets in our heavenly home.

I know the heartache of losing pets and the whole purpose of this book is to give all of you, the dog lovers, cat lovers, horse lovers and any other type of pet lovers, hope. Hope that yes, for sure, you will one day be reunited with that beloved pet who so changed your life and touched your heart for all those years. Hope that there is a better place for all of us to share a wonderful and joyful life eternally. A place specially prepared for you and me by a loving and awesome Father. One who cares about every detail of your life on earth and in heaven; even the life of your pets!

For no other reason than He loves us, and we love our pets, does He bring our beloved furry friends to our heavenly home that we might have joy in our hearts knowing we do not have to endure eternal separation. He knows how we would be broken hearted if they weren't there waiting for us.

I pray, that all of you who choose to read this book, will be very encouraged and that your heart really will be lifted when you come to understand that much of what is written here is actually what we one day will experience in heaven; even though it's expression is in a narrative form from a dogs point of view.

Let your imagination and your creative abilities, take you to a new place, a higher realm, a wonderful and joyful experience, where hope and pure love exist. It's a place where we one day will live if we choose the path that leads us to that eternal home. Let your mind drift to where dreams would only take you and open your heart to the fact that dreams do come true.

Picture yourself with your beloved pet in heavenly places experiencing the wonder and joy of seeing these things one day with them. Climb huge colorful mountains, swim in a crystal clear sea, dive off waterfalls into the colorful waters below and fly high above heaven's forests admiring the beauty of God's creation.

Let yourself enjoy the adventures of Pal and her friends as they introduce you to realms you never knew existed and journey with them to faraway places that will make your heart leap with joy; if only you are willing. Come with the heart of a child and open yourself to the beauty that was always meant for you!

Chapter 1

The Beauty of Heaven

I stood there in the magnificent brilliance of Heaven's light, totally mystified by the resplendent beauty that met my eye and all the activity surrounding me. Angels flew in circles high above, thousands of them, singing glorious songs that pervaded the celestial atmosphere. Colossal gates towered over the entrance of the bright shining city and light streamed through its jasper walls in a full spectrum of color that gleamed from its jeweled foundation. People came out to greet their friends and relatives who were entering this area. These newly arrived redeemed who had just left the earthly realm as I had, were stepping off amazing transports that were full of light and looked like bullet trains. Others were getting off chariots with their angels right next to them. Brilliant rays of dazzling color extended outwards from every direction lighting up the sky like continuous fireworks. The magnitude of this place was far beyond anyone's normal comprehension or imagination. There was no way to see where this planet of heaven began or where it would end. I was in awe. It was so bright. I had never seen light come out of everything you looked at; even the buildings in the far off distance were radiant.

Everyone was smiling, laughing or being embraced by other family members and friends. An electric atmosphere surrounded this place and joy filled the hearts of all these people, including even me. I couldn't help it, joy and love saturated everything. Heaven was so alive! Everyone I saw was beaming with happiness, so intensely that it was almost beyond my comprehension!

The most amazing thing to me at this moment was that suddenly all my senses were heightened to levels I never experienced on earth. After all, I was a dog and dogs just don't have the level of understanding that I had now. I actually knew what was going on and understood why! I was certainly about to find out much more as you will see, when you come with me on this adventure into the most magnificent place you will ever come to know. Let me tell you how this all came to be.

Chapter Two

My Life on Earth

I t was a beautiful spring day, May 11, 1964, and my mother, a Beagle, was just about to give birth. She began to show signs of labor so her human caretakers brought her to a nice box filled with blankets for her comfort. Seven cute little puppies came into being that morning, one of whom was me. We all snuggled close to our momma and immediately searched for the warm milk that her body provided. They call it instinct and I can tell you it is real even when our tiny eyes were still tightly closed. Our mom was very caring with all of us and within a few weeks we were big enough to do things on our own; so we joyfully played with one another, ate good food and took long restful naps.

Our father was a Fox Terrier which made all of us a mix between the two. I was a little female with one black eye and one white and a nice thick coat of mostly white fur with a couple of black patches to keep things interesting. My brothers and sisters had brown markings inherited from our mom but I looked more like our dad! I was particularly cute being the different one, at least that's what visitors would say when they saw me.

Eight weeks passed by quickly and one day it was time for us pups to go to our forever homes. A young girl came with her mother, took one look at me and I think we both fell in love. I crawled on to her lap and gently kissed her face. She tasted just right!

"You're going to be my puppy," she cooed gently as she held me close to her face so we could see into each other's eyes. I leaned in for another little lick and she laughed with delight. "Your name is going to be 'Pal' because you're going to be my best friend!" she lovingly whispered in my ear.

I gave her another big kiss on her cheek and knew that I had found a forever home and as we drove to my new place she held me close in her arms and I felt a whole new kind of love that I hadn't known until now!

JoAnne and I were inseparable. She took me everywhere that she went and we were well known in the surrounding neighborhoods as the girl and her RCA Victor dog since that, I presume, was who I looked like; the dog on the label of RCA Victor records!

We enjoyed all kinds of things together like visiting her friends, going for long walks and exploring forested areas together. It was there that she and her friends built forts while my friend, Boots, the neighbours' dog, and I hunted for real rabbits. In the winter we went out to the nearby golf course where all the kids would toboggan on the big hills and skate on the frozen ponds while Boots and I hunted again. Life was pretty good for this little thirty pound dog! Year after year I enjoyed the company of my loving mistress and her family.

JoAnne got older, as did I, and even though our activities changed she still took me almost everywhere she went. I remember going to the beach and enjoying the scrumptious taste of an ice cream cone she would treat me to as we sat happily in the car licking to our hearts content. JoAnne always shared her goodies with me. It made my heart so happy and certainly didn't hurt my tummy! We went for long walks with her friends after she came home from high school every day and I was always waiting on the front lawn in anticipation of that. I just loved being with my very best friend.

One of the saddest days of my life was when JoAnne had to go off to college in another city. I was ten years old by then and when she left I missed her dreadfully. I waited day after day for her to come home and when she did I never left her side. Even though the rest of the family was still there to take me for walks and play with me, it wasn't the same without JoAnne. I know she came home as often as she could but it wasn't often enough for me. I felt so empty inside and I knew life would never be the same as it had been when we were both young. No one could fill the void in my heart. JoAnne had loved me so completely and no one else could ever take her place. I guess I have to be grateful that I ever knew such love since I had met other dogs that had never known what true friendship with a human really was.

When I was thirteen years old I began having many physical difficulties. Arthritis wracked my body and I overheard that I was suffering from a brain tumor. In my discomfort all I could think about was how much I missed JoAnne. I longed for the comfort of her voice telling me how much she loved me and I longed for the gentle touch of her sweet caress.

Finally, I was in her arms once again, and after a quiet weekend together I didn't understand why she was crying into the fur on my neck. She held me close and told me how much she loved me and I somehow knew that this was not an ordinary goodbye. She kissed me tenderly on the top of my head and I had a sense that I'd never see her again. Not on this earth anyway. I didn't really understand what was happening, I just knew that when she was here everything was ok but not long after this she had to leave me again. And this time I really felt alone.

A week later her father took me to the animal hospital, a place I never liked, and as I lay there in his arms, I felt somewhat relieved that this pain would somehow end soon. I thought about all the good times that I'd had, all the joy that JoAnne had given me and wondered what would happen to me once I left this earthly realm. I wished that it could have been JoAnne who held me now. Her touch was always so comforting and her voice had a way of soothing me like no one else. I pictured her face looking down at me, smiling the reassuring smile that she always had offered when I was scared or upset and I thought for a moment that I felt her hand run softly over my body filling my heart with such love. Perhaps I was dreaming but nevertheless it felt good just thinking about her while knowing something strange was about to take place. I didn't think about much more those last few seconds and as I drew my last breath I instantly felt a peace like never before.

Chapter Three

Stepping into the Spirit Realm

Suddenly I was in a whole new place, or so I thought. I could still see myself, or my old self, lying there in her father's arms, the vet checking my pulse to make sure I was 'gone'. Yet here I stood, not quite sure of what just transpired but knowing that certainly something had happened.

"Wow," I thought, "My body doesn't hurt anymore!"

I looked down at myself and noticed all the arthritis in my legs was gone. I ventured to move my body and at that moment realized that I once again felt like the pup I used to be! I was so overwhelmed with my new body and freedom from pain that I barely noticed him standing there next to me. I turned my head upwards and saw the most beautiful man that I had ever seen. He had wings stretching upwards from his shoulders and his smile of assurance warmed me as he gently bent down and touched my head. The most wonderful feeling of what I would call liquid love poured through my whole body. I could only sigh as wave after wave of this warm love seemed to penetrate every fiber of my being. I looked up again and with great compassion he motioned to me that we were about to go somewhere else. Somehow

I knew that there was nothing to fear and as I looked back one more time I could feel my body moving forward. The room where I had just been suddenly disappeared and I focused my attention on what was happening now. This beautiful person who was escorting me then spoke ever so gently and explained to me what was going on.

"I am one of JoAnne's guardian angels," he said. "I am here to take you to a very beautiful place called heaven where you will go to wait for her to come to you. In heaven she has a home," then he chuckled. "Actually they are called mansions; they are much bigger and much grander than what you've been accustomed to on earth and you will live with her in her mansion when she comes to live there forever."

I was going to be with JoAnne again in a mansion, in a beautiful place called heaven?

"Forever," the angel repeated.

I could feel my heart beating rapidly in my chest. Even a dog knows what that word means. At least at that moment I understood. Forever! That was the best thing I had ever heard in all my life and I literally quivered with JOY realizing this was not the end, but merely the beginning of something so much greater than I could have ever imagined. I looked into this angels bright blue eyes that twinkled like stars when he saw how happy I was. He knew that I was quickly understanding the concept of what he had just said.

Suddenly we began moving very fast. I looked out over the most beautiful, sparkling, colorful stars and realized that we were travelling through the galaxies.

Again the angel spoke, "This is the journey everyone takes to come home to heaven. One day all your four legged friends and your human family will travel just like this and then live together gloriously reunited for all of eternity."

"Oh I can hardly wait!" I heard myself say.

A shocked look came over my face and I stared at the angel slightly puzzled. Did I just speak? I mean I think real words just came out of my mouth!

The angel was laughing and through his giggles he said to me, "In heaven all the animals can talk!" He went on, "Pal, you will learn so many new things. Heaven is nothing like earth and you'll have so many experiences you never dreamed of. You will come to understand things you never knew about as a dog."

That warm feeling seeped back into my body again and he once again explained. "That feeling you keep having is the love that permeates all of heaven all of the time. Your Creator, who you will meet, is the one who imparts that love. He Himself is love and all of His Creation knows Him as Love."

I was amazed. Having never known on earth what happens after death, I always wondered where my friend Boots had gone when I didn't see her anymore. Well now I knew and I kind of figured out I would see her again too.

We continued on our journey, flying through space past galaxies and beautiful stars of every color and shape. I saw a huge butterfly perfectly formed by stars and a huge blue eye that seemed to look out over the universe over everything else out there! I remembered lying on the grass on hot summer nights with JoAnne, looking up at those very stars and wondering what it would be like up there. Well now I knew, and it was an awesome sight, especially seeing them up close!

All of a sudden the brightest light I had ever seen appeared in the distance. It was huge! It looked like it was hundreds, maybe thousands of miles long and almost it blinded my eyes.

"That's heaven up there" the angel said.

I could hardly believe my eyes. The light had beautiful golden hues and all kinds of colors shooting out from everywhere like fireworks. It was a marvelous sight; almost too overwhelming to take in.

"Hey", I thought to myself, "I can see colors AND I know what they are! This is so incredible!"

The next thing I knew we landed on this huge arrivals area where streams of people were gathering. In the distance, were the most beautiful golden gates that I presumed were the entrance to heaven itself, and my escort introduced me to another angel who would take me through them and to my forever home.

"Bye Pal," he said, as he smiled and waved. I'll see you again when I come home with JoAnne. I must return to her for now but we will be back before you know it!! And I may see you in between that time .... you never know!"

" Ok, " I said and wagged my tail happily. " Bye for now. And thank you for the ride!"

He waved once again and then disappeared quickly into the vast universe of sparkling stars.

Chapter Four

My New Home

S o here I was, standing in the most awesome place I had ever seen. For some reason it was at this moment that I understood why I was here. God, the Father of all creation, loves His children so much that He brings all of their pets here to enjoy eternity with them in this wonderful place. JoAnne loved Jesus on earth and I knew she was one of His own. This was amazing, I actually had understanding, something animals don't have on earth. That in itself was astounding to me. Things began to make sense that I never had even thought of while back at home. Now I was in a brand new home.

I turned to my right and looked up at the smiling face of another beautiful angel. I loved that these angels had wings and for a fleeting moment wished I did too. They were so neat! He looked down at me and smiled with a warmth that could make any dogs heart melt.

"Welcome to heaven Pal," he announced. "This is your new home and you'll have all the freedom you want to run and play and explore and be with all your friends forever!"

I almost wanted to shout with joy and suddenly I heard this strange sound come from my being.

"Glory to God in the Highest" I sang. "Glory to the King of Kings and Lord of Lords".

I couldn't help myself; I just had to shout praises to my Creator! Beautiful ribbons of color flowed out of my mouth and formed a tapestry of light as I sang. The angel joined in with me and we worshipped for a long time.

"I sing?" I questioned, after our loud chorus ended, and without hesitation the angel replied, "Everything in heaven sings and worships God, even the rocks and the trees!"

"This is wild," I laughed, and felt my paws happily dancing round and round. Joy filled my heart and I felt like it would burst from the happiness that consumed my whole being. This whole experience was so exhilarating! The angel laughed delightedly as he watched me dance around.

"Come on," he said motioning for me to follow him. "By the way, my name is Marcus and I help to care for people's pets until a family member arrives and takes over."

I then realized that I was the first one in my family to come to this wonderful place. I couldn't wait for JoAnne to see this. "She'll be ecstatic," I thought to myself.

As I turned to follow Marcus I almost crashed into her. There stood my old friend Boots!

"Bootsie" I exclaimed! I can't believe it's really you!"

I looked her over and she too looked like a pup again, all healthy and able like the old days when I had first met her. I had only been 6 weeks old back then and she was like a mother to me already a year old herself. I remember her jumping around me all excited that she had a friend to play with now. We ended up inseparable!

"Oh how I missed you when you left!" I kind of wailed.

"I've been waiting for you Pal", she smiled. "I thought it would only be right for me to welcome you since we were such good friends on earth! You are going to love this place; there's so much to see and do. We'll stay together until one of our masters comes for us but even after that we'll see each other all the time. All the animals are friends up here. And we never will lose one another again!"

"Oh Boots, I never imagined any of this. It's so wonderful and it's really incredible to see you again. We have so many good memories to share and by what I've seen so far we will have so many more."

"You've figured some things out pretty fast Pal," Boots replied chuckling.

"And I'm really happy to see you again too!"

We nuzzled one another with affection and jumped about play fighting just like the old days.

"C'mon," Marcus motioned again. "Let me show you the place you're going to call home for now."

We walked a little further and something caught my eye. It was a rabbit. Now on earth I lived to chase rabbits, but here I had no urge to chase that cute little creature. "What's up with that?" I thought to myself, and as if I had spoken out loud Boots reminded me that all of the animals are friends up here.

"Oh yes I forgot," I said. "May take me a while to get used to that." Bootsie, as we called her, just laughed.

"Don't worry Pal, there are plenty of other things to do up here and they're much more fun. I've been here for a while and I'll show you the interesting things there are for dogs and humans alike to do. You'll be amazed. This place is far beyond anything we ever had on earth and we'll never run out of things to do or places to go! You'll see!"

I was so excited and felt very comforted seeing Boots again. I could barely wait to get started with exploring this place that filled me with so much anticipation. And now I had a friend to share it all with too.

Little did I know what I was in for!

Chapter Five

A Whole New World

Marcus, Boots and I continued our walk through the most amazing and exquisite beauty one could ever imagine. There was so much activity going on and angels and people scurried by us continually, constantly laughing and enjoying themselves thoroughly. Everywhere music could be heard and we could see people floating in the air above us. Marcus explained that when humans begin to worship they get literally 'caught up' in the worship and 'float' to the place he called the Throne Room.

"That's where your Creator lives," Marcus explained. "People go there to worship and dance and be with their Savior whose name is Jesus and His Father God. And there is a third person called Holy Spirit and together they make up what is called the Trinity or the Godhead. You will meet them soon Pal but for now we want to get you familiarized with your new home."

I noticed all the people here looked very different than on earth. Their faces glowed with love, and each person was dressed in beautiful robes full of colors I had never seen. Some had capes over their robes and they looked very regal with all kinds of gemstones embroidered into the capes; the colors dancing in the light of this beautiful place. Some wore tunics, but much more beautiful than anything I had ever seen and made of delicate materials that I don't think exist on earth. Everyone was so beautiful and so young too. They all looked like JoAnne did when she left for college. And they all smiled and laughed and sang continuously! Everybody just seemed to be having fun and they were all filled with such joy!

Everywhere I looked there was something to see. Trees, so perfect with leaves of every color, size, and shape. It didn't even seem real compared to what I remembered of earth. Exquisite flowers of every color graced the floors of heaven and some even hung suspended in the air singing tunes of worship to God. The grass was greener than ever and when we walked on it, it didn't squish down under our feet but popped right back up again; even if we stood there for a few minutes admiring all of the things around us. And the smells! (Aromas as they are known here). As you know we dogs are very 'nose sensitive,' and here all of my senses seemed to be enhanced. The aromas were amazing! Everything smelled wonderful; the trees, the grass, the flowers, oh it was a paradise for the senses! New fragrances seemed to float everywhere through the air.

As we walked a little further I saw this beautiful flower that seemed to beckon to me and as I bent forward to sniff the petals it suddenly spoke.

"Hello Pal and welcome to heaven".

I jumped back, startled, and then as the flower bent forward it smiled and began to sing!

"My, my" I said, "I wasn't expecting a flower to talk to me".

"Everything here in heaven communicates," Marcus piped up.

"Everything is friendly and everyone feels perfectly at home."

I looked at Boots who was mockingly chasing a huge blue and silver butterfly. She seemed to be almost doing a dance as the butterfly flew round about in a pattern laughing and teasing her and they moved in perfect unison along an exquisite golden path.

We continued down this pathway and came upon the most beautiful meadow I have ever seen. While on earth we used to go to some beautiful places but nothing could compare to what I was feasting my eyes on now. There were flowers and plants that were so huge and consisted of colors I somehow knew did not exist on the earth. Tall flowing grasses of every kind and color seemed to dance in the breeze and a huge crystal clear lake glistened in the brightness, looking like a backdrop in a painting. On the left a beautiful waterfall cascaded over the mountain ridge and in the distance I could see huge mansions on the top of the rocks.

To my right I noticed a lovely babbling brook which seemed to make music as it trickled over the rocks and beautifully colored fish of all sorts and sizes lazily swam in circles doing some kind of dance in the water. I could still hear music coming from everywhere and it all made a splendid symphony of sound that was very pleasing to my ears. This was so surreal to me.

Everything was alive and everything made music or such harmonious sounds that it seemed like music. Sometimes I couldn't distinguish between the two. As I scanned this meadow of beauty I saw rainbows perfectly formed over the brook. Boots ran over to one and jumped happily over it; or more correctly, on to it, and trotted right over the brook. The rainbow actually held her weight as if it were made of a substance and Marcus at this point knew what I was thinking.

"The rainbows are real Pal and you can walk on them and even slide down them. Heaven is what is called a 'supernatural place' and you can do all sorts of things here you could never do on earth."

"Wow," was all I could say. "It's all so new to me. I guess there will be nothing but new things to find out!"

"Yes," piped in Boots, "and it will take a long time before we even see smallest part of what is out there. I told you, I've been here a while and have just begun to see some of these things. Some of what we've seen right now is even new to me!"

At that moment I looked up and noticed hundreds of other dogs. They were scattered all over this beautiful area, running, jumping, chasing one another and engaging in playful and hilarious antics. Some were swimming in the lake and I then noticed several were riding down the waterfall into the crystal waters below. There were people here also and they were engaged in playing with the dogs. Some of them were riding in colorful boats with dogs sitting on the helms, their ears blowing wildly in the wind. It looked like marvelous fun!

As I watched in awe for a few minutes a new, but strangely familiar smell, flooded my senses. Memories came back to me of days spent on the beach with JoAnne and a barbeque, with delicious sizzling hamburgers flooding the air with that delectable odor. Was my nose deceiving me or was this real?

"Hey Pal," Bootsie teased. "You hungry?"

Well we had been walking a while and that sure did smell good.

"Yep, is that real burgers?"

"Sure is," Marcus said.

"Are you ready to taste the best burger you ever have eaten?"

"Oh yes I am," I replied and we all ran down to edge of the lake where a young man was cooking the food.

"Hi John".

"Marcus! Been a while. "And who is this?" he teased as he ruffled my fur and kissed me on my head.

"What a greeting," I thought to myself. " I could get used to this!"

"This is Pal," Marcus said playfully. "She just arrived and doesn't have any human family here yet so she'll be joining the group here for the time being".

"Welcome to heaven Pal. How big do you want your burger? I already know how Boots likes hers!"

Boots knew I didn't quite know how to respond so in her usual motherly fashion she laughed and replied, "Just like mine John!"

"Another healthy heavenly appetite I see," he laughed. We all snickered heartily.

After eating the best burger I had ever tasted, Boots suggested I meet some of the other dogs that were merrily playing in the distance. So we left Marcus and John and ran down into the meadow. It seemed strange to me, after just having eaten a huge burger I didn't feel full or bloated like I did on earth.

"This could be fun," I thought. "I can eat and run like the wind right after a meal!"

I felt like a pup again as we galloped through the tall grass and I jumped up and down like a grasshopper trying to see over the plants and flowers and trying to keep up to Boots. The beauty of this meadow was amazing and all the aromas permeating the air around us filled my senses beyond anything I had ever known on earth. I loved this new feeling of complete and utter abandon that overcame me as we ran and I couldn't help but think of how much fun it would be to have JoAnne here with me to share in so much happiness! All the while I felt ecstatic and that warm liquid love seemed to be continually permeating my being. I guess this was my new normal in this wonderful place.

Chapter Six

Meeting New Friends

It was so wonderful running with Boots once again. Side by side we jumped through the grass, splashed through the brook, ran in the soft sand on the beach all the while talking about the old days back on earth. We had had many good times back there but nothing could compare to what we had now. And the best thing was that we were young again; our bodies were vibrant and we could do anything we wanted without worrying about hurting ourselves. We were now, as Boots reminded me, 'forever young'.

All the other dogs in this area of heaven were waiting for their humans to one day join them too. There wasn't a breed not represented here. Every size and color dotted the landscape just like on earth. The only difference was that no one was old. Everybody was like a puppy and, believe me, they all played like puppies; running, jumping, swimming, even chasing balls that the humans and angels who were there would throw for them. And here they never got tired.

Boots and I decided to go for a swim. Boots was a Lab and loved the water; but up here I knew that I would love it too. The water was sparkling like glitter, and every color of the rainbow flickered exquisitely from the light that reflected from these diamonds that were on the bottom of the lake. Boots informed me that all the water in heaven was part of the Crystal Sea that came right from the Throne Room of God. The diamonds were from His very heart and this water flowed all through heaven in rivers and lakes and streams.

"Can we go there sometime Boots?" I asked. " To the Throne Room?"

"Sure Pal but we may have to wait for our Masters to come here first. I'm not sure."

Just then I noticed this huge dog come up from under the water with a big "crystal" in his mouth.

"Wow!" I exclaimed. The dog then dropped it and we watched it sink to the bottom.

"Hi there, my name is Jake", he said, water dripping from his huge jaw.

"How'd you get way down to the bottom Jake?" I said, and he and Boots both chuckled at the same time.

"You can swim under water here Pal, you don't even need to hold your breath...you kind of breathe under water!"

"This place is getting better all the time!" I exclaimed.

So I dove down to the bottom too and came up with another diamond, not quite as big as Jake's had been, but after all, he was an Irish Wolfhound! I found out that it is the biggest breed of all the dogs. I just had a delicate little jaw!

So Boots and Jake and I continued this game trying to see who could pick up the most diamonds. Soon there were six or seven others who joined in the game and the fun thing was we never got tired. We just kept swimming and diving and laughing at each other for what seemed like hours.

As we continued our game a young boy and girl came over and asked us to come over to a dock which was over on the shore. We swam over to see what new adventure would transpire and they invited all nine of us to go for a ride on their 'sailboat'.

Now this was no ordinary sailboat by earth's standards. This 'boat' was like a ship; one of those tall ships you see in the movies! The sails were enormous and each one was a different color, some even multi-colored, and the ship shone like it had light that illuminated from within. Peter and Sarah, who introduced themselves, bid us all to climb aboard and I couldn't believe my eyes! The interior was very ornate filled with fancy carvings that seemed to tell a story of all the places it had been. There were huge, very comfortable seats, which looked more like beds, scattered about the decks with big stuffed cushions we could lean on. The floor of this ship had a gorgeous gold lining and there were all kinds of interesting doors which led to rooms where travelers could eat and have fellowship, as I found out later. The ship was amazing and I was surprised that I hadn't noticed it dock while we were playing in the water. Once we were all seated comfortably Peter yelled out that we were about to leave.

Before we knew it we were sailing across the pristine lake. As the wind blew through the gigantic sails, they began to sing a beautiful tune that almost caught me up into the feeling of flying. Boots and I sat up at the bow where we could watch all the action ahead of us and suddenly, there, on the side of this ship was a school of these big fish gliding skillfully through the water.

"Dolphins," said Boots. "They're very playful and love to follow all the boats that go by. I've seen them before and they're very comical."

Not long after a few even bigger fish joined in and I was informed that these were called 'whales'.

What a sight! Beautiful colored skies, crystal clear glimmering waters, wild dolphins and whales jumping up and down through the water and all of us dogs sitting together our ears blowing in the wind enjoying the sights and smells of this heavenly boat tour. I thought to myself nothing could get any better than this!

Suddenly all the dolphins and whales began to sing a beautiful song of worship praising our Creator! Birds who flew overhead joined in the chorus as did several other varieties of fish. We all then joined in the song and the sea even seemed to be singing with the lapping of the waves from the ship beating a rhythm to the music. This was glorious. I couldn't help thinking about JoAnne again and how it would be so perfect if she were here with me to share in this ecstasy. "Soon enough," I thought and continued to sing a chorus wondering how I even knew it. This truly was the ultimate of pleasure and fun!

Next thing I knew our ship was flying! We were literally in the air flying over the water and then high into the heavens. This ship could do magnificent things as it twirled about the skies, the sails still singing glorious songs of praise and the ride was, needless to say, exhilarating again! I had never dreamed of doing anything even remotely close to this and as I looked over the sides I could see for miles and miles the beauty of God's creativity in this awesome place.

After cruising the heavens for what could have been hours or maybe days we gently glided back into the lake where we had started our exciting journey. We landed at the dock and bid farewell to our new found friends and as we put our feet back on the ground I felt like I was still flying. What an experience this was! I had never imagined such marvelous fun! All the other dogs and the humans that were with us followed us off the ship and everyone was laughing and sharing the adventure with others who had come to the dock. Some of them, I noticed, ran up to the deck of the ship and called out to us to watch them as they too were heading off for a new adventure out on the open sea! It was all so marvelous! No one had to worry about time or where they were going next. Life just continued on in an exhilarating fashion one good time after another! I couldn't think of anywhere anyone would rather be!

Chapter Seven

New Adventures with Old Friends

"That was so awesome Bootsie!" I exclaimed. "What an amazing place this has turned out to be!"

"Yes," replied Boots, "You haven't seen anything yet! There is so much more to see and do, just wait! Heaven is huge; far beyond our imagination."

"So what do we do now?" I asked.

We began to walk through the meadow again and I wondered where it would lead us. As we travelled along heaven's long beautiful pathways, it seemed everyone knew us. I found out that here everyone actually does know you, is nice to you, and even love you and invite you into their mansions. They feed you, play with you, and talk to you.... now that was new! Imagine, talking with humans! All the animals are friendly to one another too and everyone gets along famously. My heart was constantly filled with joy.

Everywhere we went there were huge awe-inspiring mansions. They were all constructed with light which was hard for me to under-stand seeing they were solid and they shone with such intensity that sometimes they were hard to stare at. Some were so ornately decorated with gemstones of every color and size that they reflected in the light forming fabulous rainbows. Properties were bigger than the parks we used to go to on earth and if there was a pool it had slides and waterfalls and all kinds of impressive gardens and structures surrounding them.

Everything was huge by earthly standards; and many of these properties had animals I had never seen before. Boots said they were lions and tigers and elephants and giraffes and all kinds of others that I would eventually learn about. They were all friendly though and many of them greeted us as we walked by. People could be seen everywhere engaged in the activities of heaven yet they always had time to give us a pat on the head, ruffle our fur, or even give us a treat.

Soon we were walking down one of the golden streets. This area looked more like a city and I noticed a bunch of children gathered around a friendly street vendor. I looked at his sign; just now realizing I could read, and it read 'ICE CREAM.'

"Boots, that's my absolute favorite!" I almost sang! "Let's get some!"

While on earth, JoAnne used to take me for an ice cream cone and I remembered closing my eyes as I licked delicious banana ice cream from the cone she held up to my mouth. I almost started to drool thinking about it when a young boy bent over and asked me, "What flavor would you like"?

"Banana," I blurted, and before I could count to three, a dish of banana ice cream was sitting in front of me. Oh my, was this stuff good! It even tasted better than I ever remembered and I joyfully licked the bowl dry. Boots didn't do so bad herself and wolfed down a bowl of strawberry and vanilla.

"That was amazing Boots, I so love ice cream!"

"There's more where that came from," she laughed.

We began walking again and, as we passed another huge mansion, a young golden Lab came bounding up the pathway wagging his tail wildly and yelling out, "Boots, Boots!"

"Is that Jacques?" I asked, almost unable to hear the answer, since this dog was yelling so loud. She didn't have to answer. When he finally got right up to us I knew instantly it was.

"Hi Jacques," Bootsie smiled, and the two of them jumped all over each other playing and laughing and acting altogether silly.

Jacques was Bootsie's brother on earth and they were next door neighbors all their earthly lives. Their masters had been best friends and often Boots and Jacques did all kinds of things together with them.

Finally Jacques looked up and instantly recognized me.

"Pal, you made it here too! Welcome to heaven and welcome to my Masters mansion."

"Thanks Jacques, it's been a while."

I looked up the long winding pathway to the mansion and noticed gardens that were on either side that were filled with every kind of flower you could ever imagine.

"C'mon you guys, come and see the place."

We began to walk up toward the 'house' and I noticed what seemed to be some sort of construction going on.

"The mansion is still being constructed," Jacques said. "My master isn't here yet either but every now and then I visit to see what's being added. There's a room just for me with a huge king size bed so I can invite my friends over for doggie parties. Out back there all kinds of play areas for me and my friends, a pool, a river, and waterfalls we can slide down."

"Pretty neat place so far Jacques," I said.

"So what are you two up to?"

"Just showing Pal around Jacques. Would you like to join us? I want to show Pal that very 'special place' but I want it to be a surprise."

"Great!" Jacques retorted. "You know me, I'm always up for a fun time and THAT place is extra fun! By the way, I found a shortcut that will take us there almost instantly".

"Ok you lead the way then," Boots replied.

I was a little excited to see where we were going. Everything here was special as far as I was concerned and I gladly followed the two of them as we made our way to the back of Jacques huge property.

"Right here," Jacques motioned.

There was a beautiful golden door suspended in mid- air and Jacques gently pushed it open with his nose and we all went through. My eyes went wide as I beheld a scene that I never expected to see up here. I stood in awe then took a few steps onto one of my favorite things on earth.......SNOW!!!

Chapter Eight

Winter Wonderland

I t was spectacular! We all loved snow on earth and here was a whole town; with mountains and waterfalls, a huge frozen lake where all kinds of people were skating, mansions with huge ice slides that wrapped around them and snow falling everywhere. There were huge hills we could see in the distance with children and adults on every kind of sled and toboggan imaginable. All the trees were embellished with lights of every color and some of them even had real stars that glowed with such intensity they could be seen for miles!

Everyone was enjoying themselves, laughing and engaged in fun in this winter wonderland. The aromas from this place were unlike anywhere we had been yet and my nose twitched back and forth trying to distinguish what delectable flavors permeated my senses.

"Gingerbread," Boots said. "That's one of the aromas you smell. We didn't really eat much of that where we came from but it's in abundance here. Wait till you taste the cookies!"

"And chocolate," I laughed. "I remember that smell!"

"Yes, everybody here loves hot cocoa and all the shops have it," Jacques mentioned with hesitation. "It really is too hot for my liking but it does smell great. The kids really seem to love it especially after tobogganing."

We stood there for a while just taking in the scenery and then suddenly looked at each other, and simultaneously, began to run wildly in circles in the snow tossing it up with our noses, running and jumping and playing; all the while laughing hilariously. We ran with abandon to the hills of snow and memories of tobogganing on the earth flooded my mind.

We used to have so much fun in the winter and always stayed out for hours; our masters on the hills and Boots and I hunting for rabbits in the bushes. Every now and then we'd take a ride but back on earth we were both more interested in doing what dogs did. Hunt!

"Jacques, over here," I heard a female voice call out.

A young girl about twelve years old was calling him. Jacques ran to her and smothered her in kisses obviously recognizing a good friend.

"She always takes us on toboggan rides," Boots said. "Her name is Jenny and she really loves Jacques. Her dog Pierre, looks just like him, so she kind of favors him too."

At the top of the hill I could make out another Golden Lab so I presumed that was Pierre. He was busy playing tug-of-war with another dog and as I watched I could see they kept sliding down the hill. Then they'd run back up, all the while tugging on what looked like a rope toy.

"So what is this wonderful place anyway Boots?"

"They call this Christmas Town Pal," Boots replied, "because it always looks like Christmas. Everyone here constantly gives each other, and, everyone who visits, gifts. This is where they celebrate the birth of the Savior Jesus. There always is some kind of celebration going on here and everyone is so happy and friendly. Jesus comes here often; we might even see Him. He is the most wonderful and loving person you will ever meet. He is our Creator!"

"Oh I hope He comes Boots. I so want to meet Him."

Almost as soon as I had said that I turned around and there He stood! He had the most beautiful warm smile on His face and His blue eyes danced with love. He bent down and took my face in His two hands and I thought I would melt. I had never felt love like I was feeling right now. He ruffled the fur around my neck and spoke ever so softly, "Welcome little one."

He smiled again and stood to greet the crowd who had now gathered around Him. It was obvious everyone loved Him dearly.

"Jesus, Jesus!" all the children yelled.

I was speechless. So this was the Creator! My body still felt warm from His touch and once again love permeated my whole being. Only this time it was much more intense.

"Isn't He wonderful," Boots whispered. "He loves all of His creation."

A serious look came over her face and she quietly said to me, "Jesus is known as the Savior of mankind because He gave His life for them on earth so they could come here to heaven with Him and His Father. He left heaven to make a way for all of us to come here. There is no way for people to get here unless they believe in Him. It's all quite amazing to me. Everyone loves Him so much and they are constantly expressing their gratitude to Him for His ultimate sacrifice of love."

He turned again toward us and gave Boots a pet of approval and love. Boots leaned against Him and let out a whimper of joy. Then He motioned to the children and they went off to share some cocoa and cookies.

"Boots, this is amazing, Jesus is so wonderful ! I never knew I could feel like this. I can feel His love go right through me!"

Waves of love still washed over me as I stood in awe of this Love that rolled off of Him like rivers of water. It was so far beyond anything

I had ever experienced. I could understand now why JoAnne had chosen to love and serve Him. I had her to thank that I was here awaiting her arrival.

Everyone in Christmas Town came to the center of town to see Jesus. You could hear laughing everywhere and this was surely the height of everyone's happiness in this place. There was a gaiety that filled the very atmosphere and no one felt left out; not even us.

"What an experience," I thought to myself, "and this is just the beginning of forever!"

Jesus then danced with the children in the town square. He held the little ones in His arms then grabbed the arms of the older ones and twirled around, all of them laughing with delight. They had so much fun as music constantly played and everyone joined in the party with their beloved Savior. Jubilation just permeated the atmosphere and everything that was alive including the animals and trees sang and danced in worship losing themselves in the wonder of the moment. This continued for a long time and then everyone decided to have something to eat.

We went into a lodge where huge tables were filled with delectable foods like I had never imagined. Everyone sat down and thus began a wonderful feast. There was such unity in the fellowship and love and laughter once again filled the air with such joy that I thought I would burst!

Jesus was of course the center of everyone's attention, and He talked to them with such tenderness and love that you could actually feel His love. It was so amazing being in the company of Someone so awesome.

The party went on for quite some time with jokes and laughter and after everyone had their fill, Jesus stood up hugged everybody and bid them farewell until next time! The children all followed Him to the edge of town then waved to Him bidding Him to come back real soon! Of course He said He would and then disappeared through one of those golden doors that floated in the air like the one we had come through.

Not long after, all the winter activities started up again. Boots and Jacques and I ran up to the top of the hill where several young people invited us for toboggan rides. What fun it was!

These hills were way bigger than the ones I had gone to on earth and it took a while to get to the bottom not to mention the speed was far greater too! The kids always held us tight although I found out later, up here, you couldn't get hurt even if you fell off. Now that was reassuring! We even chased the sleds down the hills racing with them trying to see who was faster! And we never tired!

After many trips up and down the hills the three of us walked back on to Main Street and went into some of the shops where people shared stories with one another and cookies with us. I had never tasted gingerbread that I could remember; and these cookies were delectable. No matter what store we entered, goodies awaited and we all filled ourselves beyond satisfaction. We never had to beg and hope for a treat here. They were readily offered to us constantly by everyone!

"Let's go sliding," Jacques excitedly said, and began to run to one of the huge mansions near the hills. Boots and I followed barely able to keep up and before we could get there Jacques had already climbed to the top of an ice slide and, with all four paws braced for the ride, he slid down yelping with joy!"

"Yippeee!" he yelled. "This is awesome!"

"This is one of Jacques favorite things," Boots laughed, and we watched as several of the children slid down behind Jacques.

"Wanna try?" I heard a young boy ask. "It's tons of fun. You can sit on my lap if you want," seeming to know this was my first time seeing anything like this.

I looked at Boots who smiled reassuringly.

"Well ok but you have to hold me tight".

"No problem, I'm Peter and you are?"

"Pal".

"C'mon Pal, you're going to love this".

We climbed up at least a hundred feet, and as I sat on Peter's lap he yelled, "Here we go!"

We flew down the slide and I yelped with glee!

This was better than chasing a rabbit! Peter held me as promised, and when we got to the bottom I motioned to Boots to come on back up with me. Jacques had already gone down several times and raced with the kids back to the top joyfully riding this slide over and over.

Boots ran right behind me and we spent a good long time sliding and racing with each other and all the kids back and forth from bottom to top. Everyone laughed as we played and I couldn't think of any happier moments in all of my life! Each activity here in heaven seemed more fun than the last. It just got better and better!

A while later one of the little girls, who looked to be about eight years old, called Boots, and Jacques and I over to one of the mansions and asked if we'd like to join her for dinner.

Sarah, as we found out her name, lived with her parents in the most beautiful mansion I had seen so far. All around the outside of the mansion were glittering colored lights; around every door, window and all across the top and sides....the whole house was outlined with beautiful lights. It was so warm and inviting and as we entered the front door and met her parents that feeling just emanated throughout the whole house.

I noticed that everywhere here in heaven love permeated the very atmosphere and no matter who we met or where we went everyone was full of love and always made each other feel loved and welcome; even the pets! This was indeed an awesome place and I was glad that this was going to be FOREVER! That was the best part!

Sarah and her parents, Michael and Katherine, loved dogs. Several of them lived in the house; twelve, it turned out, and Sarah took the time to introduce us to each one. There was such a variety of breeds here, that it dispelled all notions to me that owners only stuck with one favored breed on earth. There were however three Labs; and as I later found out, those, were always JoAnne's favorite in her later years after me.

After the introductions, the dogs all went to a huge lavishly decorated room filled with pictures of all of them and the family and memories of things they had done on earth. Lined up on a beautiful table with a bright red tablecloth with pictures of dogs embroidered skillfully within, were golden bowls filled with hot chicken, potatoes and even gravy and some colorful vegetables, which I always loved (but the chicken was the best)! The bowls were situated on small pedestals made of gold; each one the perfect height for each dog so we didn't have to bend over to eat from where we were sitting. Next to these were silver bowls filled with the best smelling water that seemed vaguely familiar.

"Water from the Crystal Sea," Boots piped up. "All the water from heaven is from there."

"Ah yes," I remembered the fragrance from the boat ride and all the swimming we had done earlier.

We all somehow knew to give thanks for our food and proceeded to eat the scrumptiously delicious meal. Then, to my surprise, when I licked the bowl clean, it disappeared!

"Hey where did that go?" I asked almost shocked.

"Everything just disappears up here Pal. Never have to wash the dishes!" a hound named Elsie said.

"The humans love that aspect of heaven, no waste, no clean up," piped in Max, a German Shepherd.

"Just walk away when you're done!"

"Wow," was all I could say. "At least they didn't disappear before you were finished licking them!"

After dinner the other dogs invited us to their 'pad at home', as they called it. We walked to the back of the mansion and entered a huge room with every kind of dog toy, huge, very comfortable looking couches and beds, and all kinds of areas that were divided for different types of ' doggie games'. A huge window opened out in the back of this room and we had a view of Christmas Town, the mountains, and the frozen lake still filled with skaters.

We all sat around on the big couches and shared our earthly and heavenly experiences; and listening to all the stories, I realized there was a lot more to see and do in heaven. I could feel the anticipation growing as I drifted off thinking about what we would do next.

Chapter Nine

Roller Coasters and Other Surprises

After some 'lazy time' at Sarah's house, Jacques suggested we go to another fun place. I never knew Jacques to be such a wild boy down on earth. He had always been tied up to a long clothesline on a rope. He never had the freedom to roam around with the kids like Boots and I had. So now I think he was making up for lost time!

"C'mon you guys," Jacques barked. " I know a great place you're going to love."

As we walked through the golden streets of heaven; the streets there are all made of gold and if you stare down you can see the reflection of yourself in them, we saw sights I never saw on earth.

For one thing there were angels everywhere. All the people in heaven seemed to have their own angel, or angels, that stayed with them all the time. They all did things together like a big happy family and it was actually fun to watch them all laughing, singing, playing, eating....it never ended.

There was constant activity everywhere. There were people going in and out of all the mansions visiting each other, bringing gifts, sitting in lavish gardens, and playing games, some of which I had never seen on earth.

The kids were the most fun to watch. Some of them moved about on what they called 'hover boards' which later became a concept in some of earth's movies. They could hover in one place or fly around at speeds that were astounding. Some of the older kids, who looked like teenagers, could actually make these boards go upside down and fly in huge circles around each other. They'd fly over the tree tops then race over the hills and back to the golden streets; all the while doing loops and yelling with glee at one another challenging each other to more daring antics. And the funny thing was, they never fell off!

I saw other kids travelling around in these huge bubbles floating through the skies of heaven and when they wanted to get off somewhere we'd hear a pop; the bubble would burst, and they would hop out at their destination! It was so cool.

There were all kinds of very different modes of transportation from cars, which we were used to, to what looked like space ships on the cartoons we watched on earth. There were ships that sailed and ships that flew. A lot of people rode horses and some of them flew too. It was all so amazing.

I rather liked the old fashioned horse and buggy rides that passed by us on the streets, and suggested to Boots and Jacques that we hitch a ride for a while. Jacques moaned at the thought of moving so slowly, but humored me since I was new. He sat in the front with the driver so he could keep his eye on things and direct the driver to where he should go.

"Want a little treat Pal?" Boots asked, and as quickly as she had said it, some delicious smelling cookies appeared.

"Wow, does that always happen?" I said with a look of pretended shock on my face.

Boots just laughed and we gobbled down our cookies with zest.

As we continued riding in the buggy I could hear what seemed like yelling in the distance. We got closer to the noise and I could hear very loud screams and hilarious laughter that echoed throughout this park-like place.

"We're here," Jacques said, as he jumped from the top of the buggy, almost flying himself. "This is the amusement park and all the screaming is coming from the roller coaster".

I followed Jacques as he ran toward the huge gates which were open for all to come in. Boots just laughed and quickly followed behind.

There were huge mansions all along the roadway to the park and even some of them had rides on their properties. They were enormous mansions and I was very curious about what was in some of those.

"Hurry up," Jacques yelled, trying to be heard over the screams that were now much louder.

As we turned slightly left on the winding road I finally could see what Jacques was so excited about. He really was into major adventures!

There was the biggest, highest, most grand roller coaster you could ever imagine. I could barely see the top where it started but I could see the 'cars' practically flying through the air at breakneck speed. People and angels were riding together in ecstasy; their arms up over their heads screaming at the top of their lungs then laughing uncontrollably when the cars flew off the track, flew through the air, and landed on another track!

I stood there with my jaw hanging and shook at the thought of what that might feel like. I did notice, however, that there were dogs and cats sitting on the laps of some of those people and they looked like they were having the greatest time. I was a little taken aback at all this when Jacques motioned to us to climb up to the boarding area.

" I don't think I'm quite ready for this," I said to Boots as I backed up to take another look.

"This is way beyond my comfort zone!"

"You're in heaven," laughed Jacques, and you can't get hurt or die here. Remember? You already did that on earth. That's how you got here!"

"He's right Pal," Boots gently cooed. It's actually really fun and one of the angels will hold you. They always help the animals on these rides!"

I looked around with slight trepidation then decided to try this out. I still wasn't really sold on the idea but once we got to the boarding area there was no turning back. I looked for a seat and one of the angels motioned me to come sit with him.

"Hi Pal," he knew my name. "I'm Roger, and you are about to have the ride of your life."

That was exactly what I was thinking, though I said nothing.

"Hi Roger," and I thought to myself again that he better not let me go.

"You'll be fine Pal," he smiled and as the cars began to move he said, "I guarantee you're going to love it."

Boots and Jacques were in the car ahead of me with two other angels and suddenly we began to move upwards. We must have climbed four hundred feet and WHOOSH! We were travelling so fast I could no longer see the ground below. Up again, round in circles, upside down and then we flew right off the track and on to another one down below. Everyone was screaming! I could hardly breathe but then Roger, who had his strong arms around me, pulled me closer and laughed the heartiest laugh that I think it must have been contagious.

Suddenly I began to relax and laughed along with him actually enjoying the air flying through my fur. I think I must have been a sight because I could feel my ears flying almost straight behind my head and I caught glimpses of Jacques with his mouth open and his jowls flopping wildly in the wind. We flew around the heavens on this monstrous machine for what seemed to be about half an hour earth time.

Finally, it slowed its pace, and returned to the boarding area that was full of new people waiting to ride. I jumped out of the car, and still laughing, thanked Roger for his assistance on the ride. He waved and turned to get back on.

"What a rush!" I exclaimed.

"Exactly," laughed Jacques. "That roller coaster is called "The Rush" and it's the biggest coaster in heaven!"

"Do you mean I just rode the biggest ride up here?" I questioned.

"Yup, and you liked it too didn't you....c'mon admit it!"

"Yea that was quite a trip if I do say so myself," I had to admit.

Boots just laughed and I spent the next few minutes trying to get 'my legs' back.

"So Jacques, where to now?" Boots queried.

"I think we deserve a hot dog, don't you think Pal?"

"Sounds good to me!" and we followed our noses to the savory smell of meat.

Chapter Ten

More Fun in the Amusement Park

T he greatest thing about an amusement park is that there is a huge
assortment of food choices. We didn't have to walk too far to find
the hot dog stand and a kind man put a bowl in front of each of us and
filled it with the biggest, roundest, hunks of meat I had ever seen, that
resembled hot dogs but tasted a whole lot better.

No food in heaven tastes like I remembered it on earth. It was all
so flavorful and the colors alone of every food would whet anyone's
appetite because it made everything look so good.

We finished our bowls of meat, licking them dry, and again the bowls
just disappeared! This was so funny to me and I thought to myself that
it would take a while to get used to all these new ways. It seemed so
strange, but there is no waste and no cleaning to do in heaven; so this
actually all made good sense!

We then walked around for miles it seemed, checking out all the
sights and sounds of this endless park. There were hundreds of rides,
some of which I had never seen; and the food never ran out. We had the
time of our lives trying all kinds of different goodies and never even felt
a bit sick riding even the wildest rides in the park right after eating!

We came upon one very interesting ride that I remember seeing the likes of when JoAnne would take me to fairs on earth. It was called a merry- go- round on earth; and usually kids rode plastic horses that moved up and down as the whole ride went in circles. Up here it was totally a different story.

This ride was huge. You actually rode real horses that flew around and rose high into the skies; then they dove down and flew a few feet off the ground. It was awesome to watch as children shouted with glee when they flew about on these beautiful creatures. Who would have ever thought?

Some of the other rides we tried out were so high up that you could barely see the ground as you rose to the tops and then wildly flew to the bottom with a rush that would leave you breathless. It was all so much fun!

There were many other areas in this colossal place where you could have picnics and try out all kinds of different foods. You could listen to concerts that featured every kind of music and many of the people and angels joined in the bands and were the actual featured players in these concerts.

Angels and people alike 'crowd surfed' at these concerts and you could hear shouts of joy as each one flew over the crowds. Everyone was so happy having more fun than you could ever imagine.

In other areas there were small lakes where you could go boating on every kind of boat imaginable. There were even bumper boats that the kids loved, and you could hear shouts of joy and ecstasy as people raced around the lake having the time of their lives. It was awesome to watch!

There were kids and adults alike waterskiing and flying off water ramps that would make your hair stand on end, yet no matter how high or dangerous looking the ramps were, no one could ever get hurt. This was the joy of heaven's experiences; everything was fun!

Boots and Jacques and I finally decided to take a rest and lay happily in the grass eyeing the wildlife that played with one another off in the distance. There were deer with little rabbits riding on their backs, bears and lions romping through the taller grasses playing games of chase with each other, and all kinds of other animals; every one having a good time. This was truly an amazing place and we all sighed with pleasure watching this array of activity.

I could hardly believe that I had the honor of coming to such an awesome place and I knew that I had never even dreamed of anything near this wonderful while on earth.

"Hey," said Boots, "How would you like to see JoAnne, Pal?"

"What?" I gasped? "Is she here?"

"Not exactly," Boots replied, "but I do know a way we can see our masters from heaven."

"Really?" I said excitedly

I couldn't imagine seeing her again so soon. Even though I'd only been here for a while there was still a longing in my heart for her and my heart leaped at the thought of seeing her now!

"So how do we do this Boots?" I questioned with curiosity.

"Well," Boots smiled, "There are places all over heaven called 'portals' where we can actually look down on to the earth and it's just like looking down into the next room in a house!"

"Show me, show me!" I shouted excitedly."

"Ok, c'mon we'll go to one of those now." So we all got up from our little rest and started a new journey to a place I couldn't wait to see.

Chapter Eleven

I Can See Home From Here

We walked for a short time admiring all the exquisite mansions that were woven into beautiful designs like a tapestry all along the countryside. The colors were spectacular and the jewels that covered each home glistened in the light creating colorful rainbows that danced through the air and sparkled like diamonds accentuating the beauty that reflected God's creation all around. Everything shimmered with splendor in heaven.

I was almost breathless from the feeling of enchantment in these glorious surroundings. I never imagined that anything could be this splendid and harmonious all at the same time, and I certainly never dreamed of being part of something so remarkable! Yet, here I was, with my old friends, partaking of an adventure that I knew would never have to end.

We continued walking along the golden streets and off in the distance I noticed an immense golden building that towered over the other structures around it. It was absolutely humongous and the grounds surrounding it were filled with huge trees, colorful and equally large flowers, and beautiful gardens with waterfalls and streams winding in every direction.

Extremely ornate benches and chairs that were colored in wood hues, silver, and gold, and embossed with every kind of gemstone were scattered throughout the gardens. Many people were milling around talking and laughing and engaged in all kinds of conversations. As we got closer, I could hear some of them commenting on their loved ones back home on earth, and I realized we had arrived at our destination.

"This is it," Boots gently spoke. "This is one of the Portals."

We walked in the arched doorways, which were gigantic, and everything inside gleamed from the gold that encased this amazing edifice. The ceilings were so high that I couldn't see the top and thousands of people were up on a platform looking over what seemed to be a huge balcony. They were all watching their loved ones on earth and I could hear them declaring words of encouragement and prayers that would send those on earth into their destinies.

Other people were shouting and laughing and congratulating one another as they watched loved ones give their hearts to Jesus as JoAnne had done years before. This one thing brought so much joy to these people in heaven because now they knew that they would soon be together with the loved ones on earth who called on the Lord!

"We have to go up there to the balcony Pal and when you look over just think of JoAnne and you will see her...it's that easy!"

"Wow," I thought to myself. The mere size of this place was intimidating but its beauty and the excitement that emanated from all the people was enticing; so we boldly walked over to the balcony railing and, as I put my paws on the rail. there she was! My JoAnne! I could really see her and I wagged my tail with joy.

She was at a beach at that moment, it must have been summer where she was, and I could even hear her talking. The sound of her voice caused a shiver of elation to fill my whole body. I wanted to yell down to her but I knew she wouldn't hear me. She was so close yet so far!!

It was incredible seeing her face again. I realized just how much I missed her and thought of the day when she would join me in this miraculous abode.

I stood there for a long while admiring my best friend and just taking in the whole scene. I listened to her voice and let it penetrate my thoughts so as not to ever forget that sound! I could only think of the day we would reunite and I knew it would be the best day of my heavenly life.

Boots in the meantime was enjoying her own experience, as was Jacques, and we all came away feeling elated. I felt like I was floating on a cloud of happiness. By the looks on their faces I think they felt the same way and we all wandered out of the building dreamily envisioning the future with our friends.

"Now that was really wonderful," I finally said.

"No kidding," Jacques dreamily replied.

"We can come here anytime we want that's the great thing," Boots piped in.

"Well this is one place I will be visiting a lot," I remarked, and we all walked into the courtyard where multitudes of people were coming in and out of the Portal.

We sat and watched all the happy faces of the relatives and friends of those who were down on earth and somehow knew that one day they too would be reunited with their loved ones. It gave us all the feeling of joy and hope as they rejoiced and declared their love for those who were yet to come to this magnificent place. Anticipation was surely the atmosphere here and we walked away dreaming of the day we would all be reunited with our Masters. We walked back into the exquisite garden area and sat down together each of us lost in our own little worlds.

Chapter Twelve

The Valley of the Falls

Ⅰ was still feeling like I was in a dream after having seen my favorite friend, when Boots stretched out her legs, got up, and asked us if we were ready to go to another beautiful place.

"There is a place I've seen here," she started, "that is so breathtaking that you will hardly believe your eyes. The colors, the scenery, the size of the vegetation, the music; it's all overwhelmingly magnificent.

"Where is it Boots?" I asked.

"I'm not sure how to get there from here," she said, "but I've figured out that here in heaven you just have to think of a place and a road of light will start to move under us and we'll get to that place."

"Wow, I love heaven Boots, everything is so wondrous!"

Jacques laughed heartily and suggested we get started thinking about where we wanted to go. Suddenly we were moving on this road of light that appeared under our feet, just as Boots had said, and the next thing I knew we were entering a huge exquisitely beautiful valley.

Boots was right. I couldn't believe my eyes. I had never imagined that anywhere could be this awe-inspiring. There must have been a hundred waterfalls all on different levels, each one flowing dramatically through rocks and crevices and all in a variety of colors. Pink, deep blue, purple, and green waters flowed from some while others streamed in a rainbow of colors. Huge, stunning, light -filled mansions sat precariously on magnificent cliffs overlooking the falls and flowers the size of buildings caught the falling water and formed pools below many of the falls. The kaleidoscope of colors in this valley was so vibrant; everything teemed with life. My senses seemed to heighten from the glorious artistry of this 'creation beyond imagination.' The charm of this place was beyond alluring. I felt like I was in a dream that was too good to be true. Words eluded me as I stared in awe at the utter majesty of God's handiwork. There was nowhere I had ever seen such beauty.

As we moved closer, following a winding path on the valley floor, music emanated from everywhere; melodies so harmonious that every-thing in the valley and the mountains and falls above seemed to flow together as one great symphony of sound. It was absolutely exquisite. This was truly one of the prettiest places we had gone to so far.

High above us we could see many people enjoying their homes on the cliffs. These mansions, which were faceted like huge diamonds, turned in circles as the people moved from room to room and you could see that they always had a view of the falls and the valley below no matter which room they stood in. It was amazing to watch.

Each home had a diving board that extended from the edge of the cliffs and people were jumping off with zest into the falls landing in the huge flowers below, then sliding down the huge leaves into a pool beyond them. It looked like oodles of fun and Jacques, 'the adventure dog,' as I now thought of him, suggested we go up and participate in some fun of our own.

We began climbing up one of the pathways that led to a dazzling mansion filled with gemstones that glittered in the light of this glorious place and heard someone calling to us.

"Hey over here," he motioned waving to us from above.

It was a young boy and as we came to where he was standing he introduced himself as Jack.

"Hi there, welcome to my dad's mansion," he smiled happily.

"Are you from around here?"

"We're just visiting for now," Boots replied.

"We want to slide down those waterfalls," Jacques excitedly said.

"Those other people look like they are really enjoying the rides and I just love anything that is fun!"

"Well you've come to the right place uh....."

"Jacques. My name is Jacques and this is Boots and Pal."

"Well, so nice to meet you all," replied Jack.

"Come on up, my dad was just cooking up some burgers. Then we can go together and slide down the falls and play in the river below. You're all really going to enjoy it here. This is the Valley of the Falls and everyone here loves to ride the falls. It's so much fun, you'll see."

We walked over to a diamond shaped elevator, stepped in, and were taken speedily to the top of the mansion. Jack then brought us to a huge patio that looked like it was made of amethyst; it was bright and a gorgeous hue of light purple stone that looked translucent.

"This is my father David," Jack said as he introduced us to a very handsome and kind looking man.

Though this had been Jack's dad on earth, up here he looked like a person around twenty-five years old.

"Pleased to meet you David," we all said at once. That brought out a hearty laugh from all of us.

"How 'bout some burgers," David offered.

"You guys look hungry," he laughed, knowing full well no one really got hungry in heaven. Here we just ate for the mere pleasure of eating. It was like a perk of heaven!

"Well we never turn down a good burger," Jacques drooled.

So we all sat down on the rocks, overlooking the lavender colored water flowing through the crevices over the top of their mansion and forming a huge waterfall down below. We eagerly chowed down those delicious burgers and talked and laughed and shared all of our adventures with Jack and David as they told us of some of the places they had seen since they arrived in heaven.

There were many things we had not seen yet and we knew it would be a long time before we even remotely discovered the beauties of heaven that awaited us. We had such a great time. It was such a new thing to all of us dogs, but especially me; having conversations with humans. It really was a great feeling being able to finally communicate the thoughts we only had on earth. Now we were able to speak them and it was indeed a pleasant change.

"OK!" Jack exclaimed as he jumped up and signaled that it was time for some real fun.

"Let's hit the falls!" he excitedly blurted out.

I was a little amazed at the whole idea of jumping over the edge of these massive falls which were probably three hundred feet high or more, but we had been watching others enjoying the huge plunge the whole time we had been eating and it actually looked like great fun.

At the end of the rocks was a diving board made especially for jumping into the falls. So one by one we took the plunge with Jack in the lead and Boots bringing up the rear! As I felt nothing but air and water between me and the bottom of this chasm I was completely exhilarated. I felt like I was flying and as I landed on this huge flower I rapidly spun down the leaves like a slide and made a big splash in the pool below. We all were hilariously laughing and as Boots landed behind me we swam to the edge of the 'flower pool' and jumped into the next level of the falls.

Finally, at the bottom in the crystal river, we splashed and played and chased one another in a mock game of tag. We played around for a long time and met many other people and dogs in the river. It was so joyous to partake of all these fun activities and everyone was so happy and friendly. When we all eventually got out of the water it was astounding to me that we were all instantly dry! We didn't even have to shake off and the humans didn't need towels. It was all quite supernatural indeed!

We sat on the edge of the riverbank for a while listening to the beautiful music, which never ceased, and admired the rainbows that formed over each of the waterfalls as they magnificently plunged to the river below. It was marvelous.

Cute little bunnies hopped along the grassy trails and deer grazed in the meadows blow the falls. I could see lions resting on the rocky ledges and other cat like animals graced the jagged mountainside. Flowering vines that were massively large groped their way up the rocks beneath all the waterfalls. Many exotic varieties of flora and fauna and smaller species of flowers covered the landscape like a lush blanket of luxuriant color. I had never witnessed such exquisite beauty.

We walked along the river for quite a while, enjoying the peaceful atmosphere and occasionally joined in the song that continually filled the valley with worship to our Creator. Everyone and everything loved worship and it was a natural thing to participate in, in this glorious place. To see the trees, the rocks, the waterfalls, even little diamond pebbles with faces, worship, filled me with such a sense of awe. This was indeed a sublime dwelling place and I now was beginning to feel more and more at home here.

As we sauntered along I was dazzled by the beauty of the valley and once again I noticed the glittering diamonds that filled the river below. They sparkled and formed rainbows of color that reflected on the rocks and the trees above and I thought to myself that I would never get over the breath-taking beauty of it all.

Just being in the midst of all of God's glory caused a feeling of utter joy and love to flow through me and I realized that everyone here constantly lived in this state of bliss. And again I was reminded that this was FOREVER! None of us would ever have to leave this celestial home!

A little while later David and Jack bid us farewell until next time and proceeded to go back up to their mansion. We dogs decided to continue our walk through the valley and followed the river through the winding paths that traced a design through the elaborate landscape.

We hadn't walked very far when I noticed a familiar face glancing our way from one of the rocks.

"Malcolm is that you?" I queried.

"So you remember me do you?" a very handsome white cat with brown markings answered.

Malcolm had lived with me for quite a long time on earth and then one day just disappeared and I never saw him again. I never knew what became of him, but here he was now.

"Yes of course. I missed you when you left our home. Whatever happened?"

"You really don't want to know Pal, it wasn't very good for me but I managed to survive a while. I couldn't find my way back home after I was dropped off in a strange place by our master. A nice lady took me in when the weather got cold and I lived with her for the rest of my days on earth. I always pined for my real home but I didn't know how to get back. It was very unnerving at first but eventually I settled in with the lady. She was good to me so I have no regrets."

"Goodness Malcolm, I never knew".

"No one did until it was too late Pal".

"I think JoAnne looked for me but never in the right place."

"Well we're certainly in a great place now aren't we?" I said trying to console him but knowing I really didn't have to.

"Yes, this agrees with me," he laughed.

"So what are you doing here Malcolm?

"Same thing you are," he replied. "Waiting for JoAnne. I know that I'm supposed to be with her when she gets here."

"Maybe you can come along with us then, you remember Boots and Jacques don't you?"

"Indeed I do," he laughed again. "Jacques used to chase me through his yard and almost hang himself on that rope he was tied to!"

"Not funny," pouted Jacques mockingly. "You were a big tease; you knew I couldn't go further than the length of that clothesline."

We all laughed at that comment and Jacques even sprouted a smile, after all up here you couldn't help being constantly happy!

"So where are you heading to now anyway? I rather love the atmosphere in this valley. I've been enjoying my stay here for quite a while. Cats love it here because there are so many places to climb and there are lots of us here keeping each other company. It's like cat heaven here!"

I laughed at Malcolm's description of cat heaven!

"We're not really sure where we're going next, Malcolm" I said as I looked at Boots and Jacques. "We're just walking along letting the roads of light lead us. So far we've been to some really neat places. I have a feeling it will take a long time to see even a bit of this place. But we're just going to keep going taking in all the adventures it has to offer! We've met some great people and angels and we've had so many fun adventures so we're looking forward to moving on to see what's next!"

Just then a huge flock of colorful birds began singing joyously as they perched on the high branches of the towering trees. All the people, animals, rocks, trees, even the waterfalls joined in the chorus and as we stood there listening to this melodious symphony, we too joined in and praised the God of all Creation. The music resounded throughout the valley causing an echo to bounce back to us filling us with unspeakable joy. Oh what joy! It filled your being until you felt you would burst and then started again permeating your senses beyond anything you could imagine. Music here was alive and you could feel an infusion of life every time worship started anywhere. It was impossible to not want to join in as it brought such a vibrant feeling of elation that unified all of creation.

After the chorus ended, we sat down to just take in all the joy the music had emitted. It was hard to move sometimes when worship happened because you were so overcome with the glorious Presence of God that it brought with it. You'd feel like just floating away and often that is just what the humans did; floated through the skies to the Throne Room to be with their Heavenly Father. We definitely had to make our way there one time soon.

"Well I guess we'll be heading out now," I said to Malcolm after the feelings of elation calmed down in my spirit. "Have you decided whether you want to come?"

"I think I'll just hang out here for now Pal. I may join you another time but it was sure great to see you guys again. I certainly will see you when JoAnne comes home, most likely before that, but I'm just going to stay with my friends here for now."

"Ok," I smiled and we nuzzled one another with affection knowing we'd be together again soon enough.

"See ya soon Malcolm," Boots and Jacques said in unison, and we all waved as we began a new adventure to the next destination.

Malcolm waved his paw and the three of us turned and stepped once again on to one of the moving roads of light. We were all anxious to see where we would end up next and watched in anticipation as the road moved us forward.

Chapter Thirteen

Fragrance to Fill the Senses

A s we continued our journey through the valley floating on this road, Boots noticed another one of those golden doors suspended in mid- air.

"Hey you guys look!"

Jacques and I turned to where Boots was pointing and at the same time said, "Let's go through!" We all jumped off the moving road in unison and looked at the lovely door beckoning us.

It seemed the natural thing to do so we all stepped up and as we did the door opened on its own. As we walked through, another scene of astonishing beauty overtook our senses once again.

A huge angel was standing just inside the entrance and, as if expecting us, welcomed us to an area he called the Mountains of Spices.

"Come in, come in," he gleefully sang.

"Wow," was all we could say.

We were standing at the bottom of the most majestic range of mountains you could ever imagine. The hills in the forefront of this range were carpeted with flowing grasses and flowers and we could see many different species of wildlife scattered throughout the whole area. Trees that were gigantic formed exquisite forests of color that looked like a mosaic on a perfect fall day. Their leaves which were bright orange, red, yellow, and rust colored reflected on the crystal lakes that dotted the mountainside and glistened in colorful hues along the surface of the water.

Huge beautiful mansions that blended perfectly with their vivid surroundings, were scattered throughout the mountainsides, on the lakes and in the meadows. People and angels were everywhere; some walking and some riding beautiful horses. Others were swimming in the lakes or just enjoying one another in their mansions. It looked like permanent fall in this exquisite area but with no dying leaves. There is no death anywhere in heaven and for that I was grateful.

If fragrances were the epitome of pleasure for a dog's nose then this was the place to be because the most luscious aromas pervaded the air here. Not only was there the smell of food from those who were enjoying picnics and other parties, but the mountains themselves gave off various aromas of spices; thus their name!

The three of us were joined by a group of young children who joyously encouraged us to follow them up the mountainside. Now these mountains were huge. Perhaps miles high. Most of the tops could not be seen from where we stood; but realizing that it didn't really matter, we gleefully followed our new found friends.

As we ventured upwards each level changed color and emitted an aroma of its own. The smells invaded my olfactory nerves sending messages of delight to my brain as I inhaled deeply with each step. Pumpkin pie, nutmeg, and cinnamon filled the air and with every level that we entered a new delightful fragrance permeated our senses. It was truly amazing and with all the delicious smells I began to crave food.

I guess that must have been everyone's thought because despite the laughing, running and playing all the children were doing as we climbed, suddenly they all stopped and a huge banquet of pie, cinnamon buns and a potpourri of delectable goodies were spread out before us. Everyone grabbed their favorite thing and began feasting, joyously laughing and talking all at the same time.

The children in heaven are so happy and constantly laughed and sang gloriously cheerful songs that even the birds and animals joined in. We too sang these jubilant melodies of praise to our Creator. We all danced together in circles and with one another and no one seemed concerned that we were dogs. It was if it was normal and expected here and it was absolutely gratifying to be part of such a wonderful existence.

All of God's creation is important to Him and He cares about everything and everyone in this tranquil home that He had brought all of us to. We were so thankful to be part of what had once been a mystery but was now our reality. We were all like one big happy family that had no end. Yes we were home!

We continued our journey up the mountains once again and I noticed all these people and angels and other beings that lived in heaven, running, riding horses and laughing hilariously. They were chasing one another and trying to catch each other by taking a picture with what looked like a high tech camera.

"That's one of the games they call 'hunting' in heaven," one of the older boys blurted out laughingly.

"They try to see who gets the most pictures and then they're put up on screens in the Hunting Lodge further up the mountain. We'll go up there and you can see for yourself. It's a lot of fun to watch the competition and you can get a good laugh at some of the pictures!"

It just never ended here. Everything was fun and again I couldn't help thinking about how happy everyone was. Joy was the main ingredient, so to speak, in this wonderful place! We watched the hunt for a while and had a few good laughs just being there, then we continued climbing to the next level that looked and smelled like buttered rum!

Soon we came upon a meadow between the mountains and there was the Hunting Lodge. It was magnificent and huge. The building itself was constructed with logs of light that looked like the giant redwoods on earth and had ornate wood carvings throughout. Everything blended in with the fall décor that encompassed the mountains and trees.

There were rushing waterfalls behind the lodge in the distance and I noticed the water was a gorgeous hue of yellowish orange and literally glowed in the light almost sparkling as it washed over the rocky ledges. The whole scene here was again breathtakingly beautiful and I couldn't help just standing there staring at the wonders of another of God's incredible creations.

"Let's go in," Boots suggested. "If the outside is this amazing we just have to go inside!"

"Of course!" Jacques and I agreed.

As we walked up to the front of the Lodge hundreds of people, angels and other heavenly beings were scattered everywhere partaking in all the activities that seemed to endlessly go on all around this area.

Inside the main doors, in an enormous ornately decorated room, were the gigantic picture screens. Large groups of people and angels were gathered together enjoying eating, drinking delightful fruity concoctions, and laughing heartily at the continuous flow of pictures that were being presented in living color! Some of the pictures were really funny; as everyone was trying so hard not to get caught, and the poses were really amusing to everyone who watched.

The three of us wandered into the other areas of the Lodge, impressed by its beauty and all the fabulous activities and games that were available for everyone to participate in. Anyone who came up here never ran out of fun things to do. We did the full circle, checking out every room, and once we had seen the whole lodge, we decided to continue our ascent to the top of the Mountains of Spices just for fun. I was really looking forward to the view from the top!

The children we had started out with had gone off somewhere else so we hooked up with a few men who were enjoying a hike to the top together. They were old friends from their earthly life and seemed to be extremely happy to be together enjoying this exquisite tour of the mountains. They had a couple of other dogs with them who I gathered were their dogs from earth, and they introduced themselves as Max and Juno. Max was a German Shepherd and Juno was a Sheepdog and both were friendly, as were all the pets in heaven. We played and chased each other up and down the hills, through the streams of golden water that flowed throughout the range, and in and out of giant crevasses and interesting caves. It was all so exhilarating playing all the time, having fun and totally enjoying life as we never would have expected. Yet here we were and all we could do was continue to appreciate the delightful life we now lived.

Finally, after climbing for a long time, we reached the top of these incredible mountains. Looking down I could hardly believe how high we were. It seemed like we could see for miles and miles and the view was beyond human, or dog, comprehension. It was astounding to realize we had climbed this far and even more amazing was fact that from this perspective the whole landscape looked alive. It smelled like all the aromas blended together up here; leaving an exquisite essence of spicy flavors wafting through the air that caused my mouth to incessantly water.

"My, my, this is so lovely," I spoke out loud, not really thinking about what I was saying.

"Yes, God sure has given us a precious gift," replied Boots as she stared in admiration at the vibrant kaleidoscope of color that endlessly changed before our eyes.

It was somewhat like a dream standing here having a view so awesome that you could barely find words to express the perfection that it entailed. The vastness of this mountain range alone was beyond anything earthly in size and we couldn't see the end of it even from this great height.

There were many other people up here too and I could tell by the looks on their faces that they were as overcome by God's glorious creation here as we were. Many just stood staring at the awesome beauty and then began to sing praises worshipping the One, who through all He did, caused joy and blessing to be their portion continually. It was wonderful as the atmosphere up here emanated all the love and glory of our Holy God!

We stood for a long time gazing over mountaintops and staring endlessly at the valleys below, watching wildlife and listening to the birds cheerfully singing songs of joy. I felt such a feeling of elation as I stood here with my friends admiring the beauty that surrounded me.

Here we were at the top of the most picturesque mountains you could ever imagine with trees so magnificent and colorful that words could not express the exquisite artistry that was uniquely displayed before us in this paradise. It was marvelous, just plain marvelous! It took us a long time before we even wanted to move again but finally, we slowly began our decent down the other side of mountains all the while continuing to inhale the array of wonderful aromas that filled the air at every level.

Chapter Fourteen

A New Family Member

T he one thing in heaven that's very different than on earth, is that there is no time; so it was very hard for us to know how much time had gone by on earth while we were on our adventures in heaven. It was only apparent to us that things changed when someone new would come here to heaven. It was always a delight to welcome the new arrivals because it made us aware of how astounded we had been when we first set foot in this glorious place. And everyone was excited to show the new ones around!

One day, as Boots and I were romping in the meadow where the dogs stayed, a cute little black dog, who I had never seen before, followed Marcus to the edge of the beach where we had first played with the other dogs diving for crystals.

"Hey Pal," Marcus called. "Come over here. I have someone you'll want to meet."

Boots and I both ran over and happily greeted Marcus.

"This is Jet," Marcus smiled as he introduced this very spunky looking black pup who was a little smaller than I.

"He's your brother, so to speak Pal. He also belonged to JoAnne. He just got here a short time ago."

"Hi there Jet," I enthusiastically chimed! "Welcome to heaven!"

"Hi to you too," Jet replied and wagged his tail eagerly.

"Jet was having a little difficulty realizing just what happened," Marcus said, a little smile coming over his face.

"Yes, one minute I was chasing a cat and the next moment I was standing next to the angel who brought me up here. He told me I had been hit by a car but I vaguely remember it. I thought I heard JoAnne screaming but it all happened so fast. So here I am. This place is awesome but it still feels like a dream."

"Don't worry Jet, this place IS awesome and you will see JoAnne again soon enough," I reassured him.

"I will?"

"Yes we all will but for now you'll stay with us and we'll show you around. This is your new forever home!"

"Well it's sure beautiful here," he whispered, "and I can talk!"

"It's a real plus for us up here Jet and you'll soon see how many other great things there are to enjoy! Boots piped in. C'mon we'll introduce you to some of the other dogs here!"

We all ran together over to the dock where some of the dogs and kids were diving for crystals. Jake, as usual, got the biggest ones and Jet was astounded at the size and beauty of our diamonds.

"This is Jacques, by the way," I said looking behind me at Jacques.

"Hi Jacques."

"Welcome, Jet, to our humble abode!" Jacques teased.

Boots grabbed him by the ruff of the neck and they began playing, chasing one another around the beach and through the water. We all laughed and I proceeded to introduce Jet to a few of the other dogs and kids who were hanging out at the dock.

"Wow, this place is so amazing!" Jet exclaimed.

"It really is Jet and it's so huge. We've been here a few years I guess by earth's time and we've only begun to explore some of the magnificent areas in this heavenly place!"

"I still can't believe that I'm here," he said. "Everything changed so fast. I kind of remember lying on the road and I saw JoAnne crying over me. I tried to tell her I loved her and next thing I knew I was with that angel. It all seemed very odd."

"I guess it would be when you don't have time to say goodbye," I replied, "but don't worry we will all be with her again someday and we'll live in her mansion forever and ever!"

"That's really something Pal," Jet responded. "Gives us all something to really look forward to," he added thoughtfully.

"So what was your life like with JoAnne Jet?" I asked quietly.

"It was great!" Jet replied. "She saved me from spending my life in a cage or part of it anyway. I was at a Humane Society and I heard some dogs never got out, although I didn't know what that meant at the time. She loved me and took me everywhere. I loved being her best friend and I loved running a lot! She'd take me on her bike and let me run for miles and then I'd sit in the carrier so I could rest. We lived in Ottawa for a couple of years, then we moved in with her friends for a year in Toronto while she went back to school. It was fun there. I was always with her friend Rosanne and her baby Lisa who played with me and their cat Ernie all day. After a year with them we moved to Windsor, where you had lived, and I had a nice back yard to play in. We had gone out for a walk the night I came here and you know the rest."

At that moment Boots and Jacques, now my very best friends in heaven, returned from their romp and suggested we go on a tour with Jet.

"There's so much to do here Jet and even if you play chase with a cat you can never get hurt again," Jacques playfully teased.

Jet laughed. We could all tell he was a very good natured dog and from the looks of it very athletic too. He had only been three years old on earth so he never knew what old was before he came here.

"Well I'm always up for adventures," Jet politely hinted, and with that we all began to run like the wind through the meadow with Jet very quickly in the lead!

"For such a small dog, (Jet was only about twenty-five pounds), he sure can fly," I yelled at Boots.

"No wonder he chased cats," Boots laughed.

Jet was exhilarated running with his new family and the four of us dogs ran freely for miles through meadows and streams and flowers. Suddenly a brand new sight, one none of us dogs had seen before, was directly ahead of us. Another gorgeous place for all of us to explore!

"Wow!" exclaimed Boots. "Look at that."

"Come on," I said. "Let's go in."

Jet stood there his mouth hanging open in amazement.

"We told you there's a lot to see Jet and every place is as exquisite as the next!"

"Who ever thought I'd be in such a place," Jet whispered.

"Your Creator, that's who," we all said at once, "and you'll get to meet Him too very soon!"

"Yes, I've heard about Him," Jet replied, "and I can't wait to see Him. I heard He is the reason we feel so loved here all the time!"

"That's right Jet, you'll see. Let's go in here now! I laughed.

Chapter Fifteen

Talking to the Trees?

"Well, well!" a huge boulder at the entrance of an incredibly splendid forest exclaimed. "New visitors!" he chuckled.

"Welcome to the Friendly Forest!" he said with a big wide grin, and for a moment I thought Jet was going to fall over!

"Rocks talk?" he said as he looked at us in astonishment.

"Get used to this Jet," Jacques replied.

"Everything talks or communicates up here Jet," I said reassuringly.

"Don't worry Jet, you'll get used to all the supernatural things here in heaven, it's really quite fun once you're here for a while."

The beautiful big boulder smiled and told us to go in and look around.

"Have a wonderful visit!" he exclaimed again. "After all, this is the Friendly Forest and everyone is friendly. This was a great place to bring your new friend," he smiled looking at Jet. "He'll be very happy that this was the first place he got to see here because this is a very happy place!"

Little did he know that we just happened upon this place! It hadn't been our plan but maybe someone else knew just what Jet needed to see first? Perhaps! Just perhaps!

The four of us now stood at the entrance mesmerized at the intense beauty that filled our hearts with delight. This place was literally awesome.

The trees were majestic and unlike any we had seen so far. Some of them were gold and others silver and their leaves looked like mesh gloves! As we watched we saw some of these trees come right out of the ground and proceed to walk around and communicate with people who were milling about or hiking the trails of this wondrous forest. It was so far beyond anything you could ever imagine and all of the trees and flowers had faces as did the rocks and the waterfalls!

The flowers were absolutely huge and, as we watched, some of the people grabbed their stems and the flowers, whose petals were very wide, began to fly like helicopters. Everyone here was having such a good time and as usual, for heaven, song and laughter was heard all around. The colors in this forest were so vibrant and gorgeous it almost took my breath away. As I looked at the others I could tell they were feeling the same way I was. We hadn't seen some of these colors yet and it was mind boggling to think of our Creator's vivid imagination as He painted His exquisite masterpiece in this forest of wonder.

"Did you ever see anything this beautiful in your life?" Jet exclaimed!

"Actually Jet, all of heaven is like this and every area has its own unique blend of beauty. It just never ends; everywhere we go we are blown away by the awesomeness of our Creator!" I said.

"Well this is pretty neat if you ask me," Jet quipped and we began to walk down the winding trail that led into a cozy meadow surrounded by trees and a small lake with a waterfall that turned all kinds of beautiful colors. This amazing waterfall was presently singing a melody of songs about Jesus.

The trees and rocks, the birds and all the rest of us joined in the melody and many of the children began to dance and twirl in circles getting lost in the ecstasy of worship. Soon we were all dancing, singing, laughing and just plain enjoying the wonder of the moment. It was a sight to see indeed; we were lost in the glory of our awesome God!

Once we finished worshipping in song the four of us continued our journey through the forest. As we walked down a winding path a huge gold tree uprooted itself and began to walk with us and talk to us too.

"Are you enjoying your visit to the Friendly Forest?" he asked with a huge smile on his golden face.

Jet looked up a little taken aback and Boots promptly answered the tree.

"We are," she said happily and smiled back at the tree.

"Everyone enjoys coming here," the tree continued, "we all are very personable in this forest and we all enjoy being in the company of God's children and His other creations too. As you can see there is a lot to do in our forest and we all want you to feel right at home when you visit us!"

"We feel at home everywhere in heaven," Jacques piped up, "but this does seem extra special when it comes to friendliness."

"Thus the name!" the tree laughed.

We continued walking up the trail and came to a beautiful stream filled, as usual, with the diamonds of the Father that glittered in the brilliant light emanating rainbows that bounced off the rocks and the trees. It was especially beautiful because the trees were gold and silver and the light penetrated these them making them look as though they were transparent.

There were people everywhere enjoying the special beauty and relationships with the characters in this friendly place and we talked to everyone we met enjoying the variety of conversations that never seemed to end. We watched the children who especially seemed to enjoy all the activities like riding the 'flowercopters', sliding down the waterfalls and running with the animals playing hide and seek with them and with one another among the towering trees.

"Let's eat," Jacques, whose appetite never ceased, suggested.

"Great idea," Boots agreed. "We haven't eaten for a while and I think since we are here, a picnic is in order."

No sooner had she spoken, than a huge picnic basket appeared and a scrumptious variety of food was carefully packed inside! One by one we pulled out all our favorites; roast beef, fried chicken, sausages and a variety of other goodies. Jet was totally astounded and stood with an open jaw watching us pulling out all the delicious choices.

"How'd ya do that?" he stammered.

"Same way we always do," Jacques mumbled, his mouth full of fried chicken.

"Just have to think of what you want and it appears, and wait till we're finished; it disappears and there's no clean up!" I laughed.

"Wow," Jet said as he grabbed a hunk of beef and proceeded to munch that down. "This is getting better all the time."

I watched as he almost drooled over the variety of meats to choose from and laughed as he almost seemed desperate to get one of everything before it disappeared.

"Don't worry Jet, it doesn't disappear until were through eating," Boots said as she chewed on a beef bone.

"The supply remains endless till you're through!"

"Oh ok," Jet replied a little embarrassed at his own exuberance.

A few other people and a couple of their dogs came over and joined us; each thinking of what they would like to eat and their favorites appeared in the basket. They began feasting too, all the while conversing and sharing with us all their individual experiences of their time so far in heaven.

It was always a joyous occasion sharing heavenly adventures. We could almost feel the life of the individual as they spoke of all they had seen and done and it gave you the feeling that you were there with them when it happened. Heaven was so different from earth on so many levels, and we thoroughly enjoyed every encounter we had; knowing too, that there would be endless experiences to enjoy forever and ever. It was almost hard to imagine but this was now our life and it was indeed glorious.

After we finished eating everything disappeared and I watched Jet's face as it vanished into thin air. He looked amused now and I smiled to myself knowing he was becoming accustomed to heaven's supernatural ways. Truly, this was an amazing place, and to the newcomers it really was something to be astounded about.

"Let's go for a swim," Jacques suggested.

The crystal clear waters of the brook and waterfalls were very inviting indeed and we all ran down to the water's edge and jumped in splashing and frolicking with fervent joy. It was so refreshing as we swam around and we made our way over to the falls. Children and adults alike, with their pets, and even some of the forest animals, were sliding down the smooth rocks in the falls shouting and laughing and having an altogether fun time. We took turns climbing up the rocks and yelped with enthusiasm as we slid speedily to the bottom and made a huge splash in the pool below.

"This is sure fun," Jet yelled as he daringly slid down on his back hind feet first. We all laughed as he almost sank to the bottom of the pool at the foot of the falls and came up amazed that he could actually breathe under water.

"Oh yeah, we forgot to tell you that little detail," Jacques teased.

"Woo nilly, that is awesome!" Jet sang out, and then dove to the bottom coming up again with a huge diamond in his mouth.

"Now this is what I call shiny," he mused, and set the beautiful diamond on the grass above and just stared at it for a few seconds.

"I don't think they had these on earth!"

"I'm sure they didn't," Boots replied, eyeing an even bigger one just below her feet. "These are straight from the Throne Room and are in all the waters of heaven as they are part of what is called the Crystal Sea, Jet. We'll have to take you there soon, it's an awesome place. Giant rainbows radiate right out of the water because of the light reflecting off the millions of diamonds! It's really quite a sight."

"Sounds awesome," Jet said with a grin from ear to ear. "I definitely would love to see that!"

"Don't worry," I laughed again, "we only have eternity to take it all in," and with that everyone laughed heartily.

We played in the water chasing one another and all of our new found friends. They were having as wonderful a time as we were. Finally, after a long while, we climbed out and sat by the falls gazing at the nature and all the activity that surrounded us in this beautiful forest setting.

Activity never ceases in heaven and you never get tired; but nevertheless we sat just enjoying ourselves, listening to the music which emanates symphonies of sound continuously and chatting happily with anyone who ventured to come by.

Chapter Sixteen

Visiting Mansions on the Crystal Sea

It was quite a sight watching the people who were riding the flowers that looked like helicopters and somehow I knew Jacques, the adventurer, wouldn't be able to resist. Just as I was thinking about it, sure enough, Jacques jumped up and announced that he was about to try riding on one.

"Go for it!" we all said at once.

No sooner had we responded, Jacques was sitting on a huge leaf on one of the flowers and it took off into the sky with him yelling out in glee from high above. We all laughed as the flower flew high over the forest and the falls with Jacques looking like he was having the time of his life.

"Hey that looks like a riot," Jet said and he jumped up, ran over to a huge pink flower and jumped on the leaf just as Jacques had.

Right away the flower smiled and yelled, "Hang on Jet!" and took off into the sky with Jet looking totally exhilarated.

"Boy he's really catching on fast, eh Boots," I remarked.

"Maybe it has something to do with the fact he was so young when he died and all that energy and daring just continues up here," Boots laughed halfheartedly, knowing full well by now that everything here just lived to have a good time and fear, or feeling reluctant, did not exist in heaven's vocabulary.

"Should we join them and see where we end up this time!" I asked.

"Why not? Just look at them up there! It sure looks like amazing fun!"

We gazed at the skies and spotted them in the distance among all the others who were on similar flights and simultaneously laughed at the sight. Not that it was funny, but we were filled with that awesome feeling of joy that always fills your heart here in heaven! So Boots and I got up and proceeded to grab a ride on a couple of beautiful orange and yellow flowers.

As I rose high above the Friendly Forest I was very impressed with the incredible view. The flower I was riding on was singing a beautiful song of praise and I lost myself in the melody as we travelled through heaven's fair skies. I almost felt like I was dreaming suspended in the celestial air until I heard Jacques yelling from across the skies to follow him. All of our flowers turned toward the spot where he was and we all came together flying extremely close but not touching. These flowers knew what they were doing and it was all great fun.

"Look over there," Jacques yelled as he pointed to a huge body of water.

A woman who was flying by on another flower heard him and told all of us that was one part of the Crystal Sea.

"Hey, let's go down there," Jacques motioned. "This is what we were talking about Jet!" he yelled.

The flowers were very obliging and we began descending onto what looked like a beach area with huge mansions built all along the water's edge. We could see out over the water and there were huge mansions floating on the surface of the sea too. It was really amazing especially considering the size of these homes!

The flowers landed on the beach and we all got off, thanked them for the ride and they happily flew back into the skies all the while singing glorious songs of praise once again.

"Wow look at this place!" Jet exclaimed. "I can't believe the size of those mansions out on the water. They look like they're suspended somehow!"

They were absolutely enormous and incredibly eye catching for sure. They looked like they were sitting on a column of some type and then much to our astonishment one of them began to lower into the water and after a few moments disappeared below the surface!

"Did I just imagine that or did one of those mansions just go under water?" Jet asked.

A man and woman who were walking up the beach at that moment heard his comment and laughingly replied to him that these were called Aqua-Mansions and they were suspended on huge columns that allowed the residents to live under or above the water at any given time.

"Now that is awesome!" we all simultaneously remarked, and we all began to laugh at the thought of such an awesome home.

"You can go visit any of the mansions any time," Sheila said introducing herself and her friend Mark to us.

We all introduced ourselves too and then Sheila surprised us by inviting us to her aqua mansion.

"You live in one of those?" I said.

"Sure do," she replied. "When I lived on earth I was a marine biologist and spent a lot of time scuba diving and snorkeling studying all the underwater life and I couldn't imagine being separated from the sea and all its magical life forms. This is exactly what I would have picked to live in but as you know our wonderful Father knew that; and here I am in my dream home!"

"Cool!" Jacques commented.

"C'mon everyone and I'll show you how it all works!"

We proceeded to walk on a path of light right over the water to Sheila's mansion. When we got up close we realized just how humungous these mansions actually were.

"This aqua mansion is about ten thousand square feet around," Sheila mentioned excitedly, "and every time I walk around it I get joyous all over again! Wait until I show you all the wonderful amenities these mansions offer. There is so much to see!"

She led us into a huge room filled with large circular windows and as she pushed a lever on one of the walls the mansion began to slowly sink below the surface of the sea. As we looked out the window we could see the beautiful rainbows shimmering on the surface of the water reflecting off all the diamonds on the bottom. Then, ever so gently, the windows became covered in water and all kinds of beautiful brightly colored fish and exquisite marine life were swimming within view, close enough it seemed, that you could almost reach out and touch them.

"Oh my goodness!" Boots exclaimed, "this is amazing!"

As the water fully encompassed the room, we looked up and noticed at that point that the ceiling was also made of this clear substance and we almost felt like we were in a fish bowl, only the fish were on the outside. It was truly awesome and it only got better because as the room went deeper the marine life got bigger and we watched as dolphins and whales and other large fish swam by.

"I can see why you love living here Sheila," Jacques commented.

"Wait until you see what's in the room next door," Sheila replied.

"Anybody up for a swim with the dolphins?"

"Sure!" we all agreed together, and we followed Sheila to the next room where a water portal led us to a platform where we could step out into the water to go for a swim. It was incredible. We all jumped in excitedly and six friendly dolphins greeted us and offered to give us rides through the water.

We all rode the dolphins and as we came to the surface of the sea we swam around Sheila's mansion just to get an idea of how large the outside circumference was. We were all laughing and having a grand time and as I looked down into the water I marveled at the beauty that I beheld below.

The sea looked like a carrousel of color with the variety of beautiful fish swimming around almost creating what one would imagine as a dance in the water. It was so amusing watching all the activity that lived below this awesome sea.

We finally decided to end our lovely swim and climbed out on another platform that was still above the water in the mansion. Sheila then invited all of us to view the rest of her mansion and it was indeed exquisite.

All of the rooms had wide open views of the sea; either on top or underneath the water, and every room was absolutely huge. There was a living room all done up in exotic colors like the fish that you could view from the lower windows. An aquarium, that was the length of the room, allowed fish to swim in and out of the mansion through little portals cut into the walls. Another of the rooms was done up in royal blue, baby blue and white and kind of looked like a study of sorts that had pictures of Sheila in dive gear when she worked in the ocean on earth.

The dining area was done in vibrant yellows and oranges and a huge crystal table was the centerpiece of this room. There were at least forty chairs around it all covered in different ocean themed designs. They were gorgeous! All the décor in this room looked like coral formations or seashell designs and had huge green plants growing out of them.

"I take it you love bright and cheery colors," I mentioned to Sheila and she laughed wholeheartedly saying," Whatever gave you that idea?"

We all laughed too and continued admiring all her gorgeous rooms, each filled with furniture appropriate to that room, and pictures of all kinds of places she had been and things she had done on the earth. The walls literally told the story of her life! It was so marvelous sharing all these experiences with these people who were genuinely loving and kind and who saw no difference in sharing with us than they would have with any friends even though we were just dogs. This sure wasn't earth!

"So where do you live Mark?" Jacques asked politely.

Mark had been watching us with amusement as our faces continually changed expressions with every new turn into each room.

"I live across the way in a beach mansion," he answered.

"I love the sea too," he continued, "but I prefer living on land and looking out over the water! Besides I also love animals that prefer land life so they all live on my property and we still can enjoy being near the water. I have this view of all these Aqua mansions and find it quite amusing watching them appear and disappear continually. I think these water people can't decide whether they want to be in the water or on it," he teased as he looked lovingly at Sheila.

"So cute my dear!" Sheila smirked. "Mark and I were husband and wife on earth," Sheila shared with us. "He never really cared for the water too much except to look at it and I practically lived in it!"

"So true," Mark added. "And look at this; we both have our dream homes here in heaven and we get to be very close to share all our favorite things with one another and we actually enjoy it all. How wonderful is that?"

"Pretty wonderful indeed," Boots replied. "It's all so splendid when you think of it and there is nothing but joy to share, one for another!"

"Come out to the patio," Sheila suggested, "and I'll bring out some treats."

We all walked around to the front of the mansion where a huge beautiful patio surrounded an area with real sand and palm trees, whose branches blew in the breeze, giving you the feeling you were on a tropical island. It was so awesome. There were comfy chairs all around, lush green gardens that all looked tropical too, and even a couple of hammocks where one could lie watching the activity out on the Crystal Sea.

A variety of boats and ships cruised by and everyone always waved to us as they passed. It was gorgeous and at the same time very relaxing and peaceful.

Mark hopped up on a hammock and the four of us dogs jumped up on the comfy chairs and lifted our noses to the breeze coming off the sea. The air was so fresh and always smelled sweet so it was a pleasure to our senses to deeply inhale and take in all we could.

Sheila popped around the corner with a load of fruits and other goodies that we dogs would enjoy, and offered us an endless variety of things that made our mouths water. She and Mark enjoyed a delectable looking fruit drink and we talked and shared about all of our adventures in heaven. There was always so much to share and new things to hear and we dogs sat very attentively as they spoke of their journeys and told stories of their life together on earth.

It was so wonderful to see how God enjoyed keeping everyone together here and we all realized how important it was to be with friends and family. Even we animals had that privilege being with one another again and I thought of how wonderful it would be one day for JoAnne to join us and we would all live happily ever after! The very thought made me quiver with joy!

After we all finished the goodies and gab, Mark invited us over to his mansion.

"I have some pretty cool things over there too," he laughed. "Think you'd like to see something different than this?"

"Oh yes," Sheila added to his invite. "Mark has a few things it sounds like you haven't experienced yet!"

"Well, I guess we'll definitely have to check this place out," Jacques quickly replied. "We always want to see new things."

Chapter Seventeen

A Real Jungle Experience

Wtext continuese all got up from the comfy seats and walked to the edge of
Sheila's property and once again a beautiful road of light
appeared and we paraded over to the beach area where Mark's mansion
was situated.

Though very different from the Aqua mansion, this place was no
less impressive. In fact, it was even more amazing to me because of the
way it was constructed with all of the front area facing the sea, and as
we walked around to the back, all of those rooms faced an incredible
scene like something out of Africa. There was a jungle area filled with
exotic trees and fauna that were huge and green beyond green! Wildlife
was everywhere. Lions and tigers roamed the paths, monkeys swung
happily from the branches of the trees and beautifully colored birds sang
from high on rocky perches. In the distance I could see giraffes and
elephants and other large animals mulling about. A huge waterfall and
lake glistened in the distance and we could see animals enjoying the
cool waters and playing together in this tropical paradise. It was breath-
taking as usual and Mark breathed a sigh of utter joy as he once again
walked into his mansion.

People, I noticed, seemed to re-live over and over again the ecstasy and joy of seeing how perfectly made their mansions were for them by their loving Heavenly Father. Every time we went into a home, joy would just fill our hearts as we experienced the gratefulness of every person to their Creator! It was so awesome to always feel so good and share in each other's happiness continually.

Mark we found out, had been a biologist too but of a different sort than Sheila. He had studied in the rainforests of South America and in the heart of Africa and had grown to love the wildlife there while on earth. He loved the ocean too where he and Sheila had once lived, so here he had the best of both worlds and lived close to his now best friend and together they could share in each other's passions!

It was all so amazing and so beautiful to recognize the love of the Father for all of his family and to know that each person had a perfectly prepared place designed around their gifts. He alone had known the desires of every individual heart and fulfilled them to perfection. It was no wonder to any of us that everything and everyone could never cease to worship our loving God!

Mark took us through his mansion that was filled with exotic décor and looked like colorful botanical gardens. Each room had furniture that was handsomely sculptured with overstuffed cushions to sit on, exactly what you'd picture a man would love. There were spectacular wall hangings of African animals and scenery on many of the very high walls. Huge beautiful green ferns and other plants sat everywhere in colorfully painted elongated ceramic pots.

Palm trees and a three story waterfall were built right into the house and flowers of every species and color hung from hanging baskets. Some were even suspended in the air near the walls. Huge vines twisted their way like gnarled fingers through the trees and sprouted gorgeous tropical flowers which periodically peeked out from inside the long braids of bark.

There were many pictures on the walls of journeys Mark had engaged in while on earth and a lovely portrait of him and Sheila displayed proudly in his huge dining room. There was an exquisite 'Amazon room' that made you feel like you were in the middle of the Rainforest and all of the décor of this room was finished in an endless variety of greens. Cute little lizards played hide and seek in the foliage and colorful birds sang from the tree branches. It was a sight to see!

"Want to take a walk out on my property?" Mark asked.

"We can take a ride around on one of the elephants," Sheila offered.

We all looked at one another and almost simultaneously said, "Yes!" with great anticipation. Remember, none of us had ever seen many of these animals, save on TV, when our masters watched animal shows back on earth! This was going to be a real treat!

Mark called over two of his elephants, Ellie, a huge African, and Ivory who was pure white. They were so friendly and knelt down beckoning us to climb up for the ride. We dogs all hopped on and sat down on Ellie and then Mark and Sheila climbed up on Ivory. Both elephants then proceeded to carefully rise and we had an eight foot high view from their backs of the sprawling property that looked like a jungle.

It was amazing again! The elephants took us through winding paths of vegetation and flowers we had never seen before and monkeys happily swung above us in the trees greeting us as we passed under them.

A cute little baby monkey, Mark had named Tarzan, jumped on Ivory and flew straight into Mark's arms. He cooed and hugged Mark tightly, who by now was laughing hysterically at the antics of his friend. This little guy loves me he laughed and Tarzan put Mark's face between his little hands and kissed him on the cheek!

"You're such a sweetie Tarzan!" Sheila exclaimed.

"You've stolen Markie's heart," she affectionately teased.

We all laughed and Tarzan plopped himself on Marks lap determined to continue riding with us.

We soon came to the beautiful lake area with the diamonds of heaven glistening in the light as they did wherever there was water. Many different species of wildlife filled this area and from here we could see the waterfalls. They were probably a hundred feet high with water flowing in every color. At the bottom, delicate steps were forged in the rock covered with a variety of deep green, purple and burgundy moss. Below the surface and between these steps, every color of gemstone sparkled brightly as the water swirled about in circles.

Flowers of every color and size covered the rocky ledges around the falls. Lions lazed about on these ledges along with tigers and panthers with coats as black as ebony. Elephants played in the water and impalas lazily walked around the edges amused by the antics of their friends. Giraffes walked elegantly in the distance and grabbed leaves from the towering trees as they passed by. It truly was like a scene out of a movie; only much better!

"Sometimes I feel like I'm back in Africa," Mark commented, "only the smells are different and it isn't sweltering hot!"

We all laughed, knowing full well what he meant by smells!

We continued our tour astounded by how large this jungle was and enjoyed the endless variety of wildlife and vegetation. After a long while we came to the edge of his property, as he informed us, and looked across at what seemed to be miles and miles of magnificent gardens of flowers. The colors could have filled a galaxy; they were spectacular to behold and we all sat there staring at the stunning beauty of this phenomenal landscape.

"My neighbor is my sister Angela," Mark laughed. "Can you guess what her gift is?"

Sheila chuckled and hesitatingly offered, "could she be a florist dear?" and with that comment we all laughed again.

"My goodness," I half whispered, "I have never seen so many flowers or colors for that matter in one place," noting to myself that heaven is filled with exquisite colors everywhere.

"This is just beyond beautiful!" Boots remarked.

The flower gardens seemed endless with gorgeous winding paths leading in and out of each cluster of color making it look like an exotic painting you would have to really struggle to even imagine. Yet here it was, another marvelous canvas of glory created by the Father of Glory Himself! This really did take my breath away, as did so many things in our heavenly home.

"If you ever want to send a splendid gift to someone, her bouquets and arrangements are out of this world!" Mark exclaimed and laughed heartily realizing what he had just said.

"Yes definitely out of this world," Sheila added smiling.

"Well her place sure is different than anything else we've seen up until now," Jacques commented. "Exquisite indeed!"

We looked out over the gardens for a while longer and then the elephants turned and began walking back through the jungle. As we arrived back at Marks's mansion a group of visitors were gathered on his patio talking, laughing and eating some great smelling foods.

"Hi everyone!" Mark yelled from atop Ivory. "These are some of my friends and relatives from earth," he explained to us.

Our friendly transports bent down on their knees and we all hopped off on to the ground.

"That was a wonderful ride," we all thanked Ellie.

"My greatest pleasure," she replied and walked off into the jungle toward the falls for a refreshing swim.

There was a lot of commotion with all the visitors who had come to visit Mark and Sheila and we all engaged in the fun activities that had begun to take place. There were lots of young kids there and they all ran around playing chase with us and threw balls for us to fetch, racing us to the lake where we all dashed into the invigorating cool waters and played for a long time. There was nothing but fun to be had by all and we all did just that!

After a long refreshing swim and water games we all decided it was indeed time for some food and the delicious aromas wafting through the air led us directly to the patio and tables that were set with an array of delectable goodies. We ate to our hearts content and then sat around listening to all the stories and conversations that were being enjoyed by Mark and his company of friends. It was awesome. There was always so much activity here and no one ever got bored or didn't have a great time.

Fellowship is the main activity of heaven and it includes everything from talking to worshipping, playing, swimming, hunting....you name it we did it! And it was all fun!

Chapter Eighteen

Big Waves and Pet Portals

I don't know how long we visited with Mark and Sheila. We met so many fascinating people and all kinds of species of animals and even made many new dog friends too.

In heaven, things happen in one long continuum; remember there is no time and this alone is a wonderful part of our home. You are never late, never too early, never stay too long or not long enough. Activity never ceases, neither does worship, as everything we do here is considered worship; even having fun is considered by God to be worship. Our minds have so much more capacity here and understanding and revelation is a given even for us animals! On top of all that, we are in a continuous state of joy and filled to overflowing with love. Oh our marvelous and awesome Father God. How He loves His creation!

Well, eventually the four of us decided to move on so we waved to our new friends and began walking down the long beautiful beach.

"That was sure a lot of fun," Jet remarked thoughtfully.

"Everyone is so nice and kind and fun too," Jacques added.

"We certainly will never run out of friends here," I half joked and we all laughed with much joy flooding our beings.

Looking out over the Crystal Sea was absolutely amazing and every time I did there was a new inviting scene to behold. The water glistened with rainbows of color shooting everywhere from the beautiful gemstones beneath the friendly waves. Sailing ships of every size flowed in the gentle breezes with songs of worship pouring off the magnificent sails leaving us with a sense of awe and wonder each time they passed our way.

Way off in the distance we noticed huge waves breaking quite far out in the water. As we moved in closer to this wondrous sight we saw just how humongous these waves actually were, and there, in the midst of these amazing breaking waves, we saw surfers riding fearlessly through the wild waters. It was awesome. The waves were probably seventy five to a hundred feet high and the surfers were having the time of their lives, so to speak.

"Oh no," I thought to myself. "I sure hope Jacques doesn't want to try this!"

We all just watched and cheered from the beach and Jacques never said more than "wow," so I must say I was a bit more than relieved!

We found out this area was a surf park and surf they all did. Seeing surfing on television, as I had when JoAnne used to watch it on earth, was far different than seeing the real thing up here. I was just grateful that here a surfer couldn't get hurt or drown!

It looked like absolute fun and I could tell that the poeple out there riding the massive waves loved what they were experiencing! We watched all the activity on the beach and in the water for quite some time as it was truly very awe-inspiring. This area sprawled out for miles and miles and we finally agreed to continue on after watching and chatting with numerous other onlookers wondering what we would come upon next.

I looked a little further down the beach and noticed a group of dogs and puppies gathered around a little park-like area.

"Hey guys, look at those dogs. What do you suppose is going on there?" I queried.

"One way to find out," Jet answered, and we all headed to where they were gathered.

There must have been twenty dogs and I noticed several other species of animals with them too. Cats and birds, a couple of monkeys and even some horses were further into the little park.

"What's going on here?" Boots asked one of the other dogs.

"We're looking through the portals in the park at our old homes on earth and our masters who still are down there," April, an elegant Afghan, replied.

"You mean there are portals here?" I remarked rather astonished.

"Yes, there's a few of them in this park on the ground for us animals to look through. See, over there," she pointed.

Beautiful flower gardens surrounded circular areas where we could go and look into a portal that was especially made by our Creator for the animals to see our beloved masters. I was astounded and we soon learned that these portals were all over heaven.

"Funny," I thought to myself, "that we hadn't noticed them before," but all that mattered now to all of us was that we could look down and see our earthly masters once again.

The four of us were so excited so we formed a circle around one of the portals and gazed lovingly at our beloved friends on earth. Jet was amazed, as this was his first visit to a portal. All of us stood for a very long time watching the activity of our best friends back on earth.

By this time we saw that JoAnne had another dog and cat and they all seemed very happy living together in her home. I was very glad that she had some new pets and I thought of the day when all of them too would be part of our happy family here in heaven. I only wished I could speak to them now but I knew that it just wasn't possible so I made up my mind to just soak in the love that surrounded me as I watched my favorite human friend engaging in her life back on earth.

Jet was mesmerized by the scene below and his tail never stopped wagging. I knew by his reaction that he had loved JoAnne every bit as much as I had. It was a funny feeling to realize that we could all feel the same about one person but at the same time it was very comforting to know that we had all filled JoAnn's heart with such love too. And she had given us all the love that we needed in our lives; be it at different times. Soon enough we would share eternal happiness together and one day we would all be home at last! What a wonderful thought!

"This is awesome!" Jet exclaimed as he turned his face toward us. "I can't believe how close everything on earth seems."

"It really is amazing, isn't it?" Boots cooed. "Every time I see my master I can hardly wait to see him again! It's never too soon."

As usual, after such an experience, we all were lost in our own little worlds thinking of the day we would be reunited with the ones we loved so dearly. Love certainly is a wonderful thing!

Chapter Nineteen

Mansions in the Sky

After leaving the pretty little park on the beach we headed in the opposite direction from which we had come. As we continued walking Jet suddenly yelled out, "What's that?" as he looked up in the sky, and all of our eyes looked upwards.

There, flying around one of the mansions property just above the beach, was an object shaped like a mini spaceship! We stood looking in awe and the man who was flying the thing looked down at us as he flew over and then to our amazement came straight down and landed on the beach. He opened the door of his space ship and jumped out to greet us.

"Hi there guys and gals!" he said enthusiastically. "My name is Ronnie. I saw you all down here and thought you might be interested in a flight by the way you were staring at me! Never seen one of these?"

"I've seen them in the distance," Boots offered, "but never up close."

"Me too," Jacques and I answered at the same time.

"It's new to me," Jet said. "By the way, I'm Jet," and we all introduced ourselves to him one by one.

"Well it's a pleasure to meet you and this, my dear friends, is a star cruiser and I live far away in a sky mansion. I fly around enjoying a lot of heaven from the air. I love flying. I love the view from the heights of the sky! I always l treasure the feeling of the freedom it offers me!"

"Let me guess," Boots laughed. "You were a pilot on earth."

"Well, your one smart pup," he laughed back. "I was indeed, and now I can fly around for eternity. How great is that?"

"Pretty great," we all replied together.

"So how 'bout it? Want to go for an amazing ride and visit my sky mansion? That's what I live in."

"Oh yes," we all said excitedly.

"Sounds awesome to me," Jet added. "A sky mansion?" he whispered to himself.

"It is," Ronnie quipped. "Come on hop in!"

Ronnie's star cruiser was much bigger up close than it looked way up in the sky where we first spotted it. It was so colorful and the hood of it looked like there was glitter in the paint as it reflected in the light; especially now that he was parked so close to the Crystal Sea that already sparkled from all the diamonds and gemstones. We all fit in comfortably and I was surprised at how fancy the inside actually was and how comfortable the seats were. This was going to be very special for all of us!

The star cruiser began to lift straight off the beach and suddenly with a whirl we were thrust through the skies of heaven. It was incredible! We flew high over the Crystal Sea and the rainbows that shot out from below were much more spectacular from this perspective. We could see hundreds of aqua mansions scattered over miles and miles of the sea and islands that were extravagant, with mansions that were sensational. The huge surfing waves we had just seen looked small from up here in the skies. The sights were astounding and we all felt thrilled by this marvelous ride in the cruiser.

Soon we were in a whole different area that was filled with huge three or four story circular mansions with gigantic windows built on huge columns.

"These are what are called the Sky Mansions," Ronnie said with a look of love on his face.

"I live in one not too far from where we are now. I'll take you there and you can see what they`re like inside."

"Oh yes, we'd all like to see the inside of one of these," I said with anticipation in my voice.

"Great!" Ronnie replied.

Ronnie made a wide circle and we had a view of all around the area of the sky mansions. It was awesome! I had seen my family on earth watching a cartoon called 'The Jetson's' and this place had a pretty close resemblance to it; only much more spectacular!

Ronnie pulled up to a huge sky mansion and landed the star cruiser on a platform that was constructed as a landing area. The door opened and Ronnie invited us on to the patio of his amazing mansion. We were very high up, hundreds of feet in the air I'm sure, and the view was spectacular again! We could see for miles over the skies and many star cruisers were flying about enjoying their wondrous environment. We stood there for a while on the platform watching all the activity and then Ronnie invited us inside.

The inside of this mansion was as fascinating as the skies themselves. Everything was high tech. The floors moved us from room to room and there were gadgets here that we hadn't seen elsewhere in heaven. Everything was automated in this mansion.

All of the furniture faced the huge windows and in each room you had a view of the heavens outside. There were buttons and levers on every wall and Ronnie showed us how each one had a purpose of its own. He'd push one button and a chair would turn in a different direction, or a wall would open and we'd be in another room.

We came into this huge area and as he pulled a lever on the wall the floor opened and an enormous swimming pool filled with water from the Crystal Sea came into view. Trees popped up and pottery filled with ferns rose up from holes that were in the floor making the room look like a tropical paradise. Comfortable chaise loungers came down from the ceiling and gently set down under the palm trees.

"The best of both worlds," Ronnie sighed. "My Lord thought of everything!"

"I'll say," Jacques replied, and proceeded to dive into the gloriously inviting water. We all laughed and Ronnie jumped in and joined him. We all then leaped in too and played and splashed about all the while glancing up in time to see another star cruiser fly past the giant windows. It really was phenomenal!

Ronnie finally climbed out of the pool and called for us to follow him. We all climbed out and as usual, were instantly dry, and followed Ronnie to his huge living room on the level above. There were about thirty people up there all visiting and having a great time of fellowship with one another, laughing, joking and singing together while a couple of guys played guitars.

Fellowship in heaven was always fun and we met so many new friends wherever we went. Everyone loved each other and always wanted to know one another's story. The party at Ronnie's grew as more visitors and a few of his relatives came by and food and fun flowed generously for all of us to enjoy. It was quite a sight this party in the sky!

After what would probably be days by earth's time the four of us decided to move on to a new destination. Everyone either said or waved goodbye to us, gave us a pat on the head or a little hug and made us promise to come by again. We took an elevator from the top of Ronnie's mansion and down to heaven's streets we went.

"That was sure a great time," Jet remarked, and we all agreed.

It was always nice to feel so welcomed no matter where we went or what we did.

It had been a while since we had seen Marcus and the other dogs back at the meadow so we decided to take a little trip there to see if anything new was happening. We stepped on one of the roads of light and before we knew it we were back, smelling the familiar aroma of John's cooking. It seemed to me John continually cooked; as he absolutely loved creating new delectable creations and he certainly never ran out of willing samplers.

We were greeted with excitement by all of our friends, introduced Jacques, who hadn't met the group yet. Marcus was very curious as to where we had been and what fun things we had done.

So we all sat down munching on the great foods John set before us and shared all our adventures from the far reaches of heaven. Some of the other dogs and people shared their exploits too and it amazed me that we had all had such variety of experiences; which made me realize just how vast our home actually was!

After sharing our stories we all decided to take a dip in the lake and play some water games. We all loved the water, and wherever there was some, you could find us enjoying a refreshing swim. And there is lots of water in heaven!

As we were playing our favorite 'get the biggest gemstone' game, a cute little girl cozied up to me and whispered in my ear, "Wanna go somewhere really neat with me?" and then she smiled a suspiciously cute little smile!

"My name is Maureen." she whispered, then let out a hearty laugh.

"Where is it you'd like me to go with you?" I asked with curiosity.

"Just follow me and I'll show you something really neat."

"Well, ok," I answered. "Can my friends come too?"

"Sure," she replied. "They'll love it too; everyone does!"

Then she called out to four of her friends who all looked about ten or eleven years old who had been playing on the beach.

"C'mon you guys, we're gonna show these dogs a good time! They haven't even visited our favorite playground yet!"

I wondered what they were all talking about but I could see the excitement on their faces so I called Boots, Jacques and Jet and we jumped back onto one of the moving roads of light with the children leading and laughing all the way!

Chapter Twenty

Is This For Real?

As we rode the path of light, Maureen introduced her giggling friends to us one at a time. There was Patty, Karen, Kathy and Abby; four of the cutest and happiest little girls you could imagine. They seemed very excited at the prospect of taking us to this secret place and teased us incessantly about the new kind of fun we were about to engage in.

"This will be more fun than anything you've done yet," Kathy laughed.

"You'd never guess what it is....I don't think anyone would ever think of such a place except Daddy Himself; oh how He loves us kids, just wait and see," Karen piped in.

Jacques was getting very excited, his tail wagging wildly giving away his emotions. He so loved adventure; but then again we all were always anticipating new fun wherever we went. It was becoming normal to expect it; there was no such thing as disappointment here!

Suddenly we could hear oodles of children exuberantly laughing and yelling in absolute glee. As we rounded a hill on our road of light there it was! Miles of brightly colored JELLO everywhere! All of the children jumped off the road and ran toward 'JELLOLAND' shouting and laughing all at once.

I thought my eyes were deceiving me it was so amazing! Jacques ran right behind the girls and I watched as he bounced almost six feet high when he jumped on to the fiery red jello at the edge of the road. The girls were all bouncing around laughing with joy as they watched Jacques who was trying desperately to retain his balance.

I looked across the landscape at miles and miles of jello; it went on as far as the eye could see. Every color; red, green, yellow, blue, purple, orange, and many other colors not normally associated with jello. There were jello houses, jello rainbows, the pathways and countryside, the flowers and trees all made of jello! The trees even had whipped cream tops and I could see kids climbing them to dip their hands into the rich fluffy cream! I watched as the children and adults too, jumped unrestrainedly bouncing to heights that really blew me away. I could see that you could eat the jello as you played and jumped, and it would automatically replenish itself right away. It was indeed a sight to behold.

"C'mon," Jacques yelled to us. "This is a blast!"

Maureen yelled out to us; "I told you you'd never imagine this!"

She was certainly right. Not one of us would have ever thought of this place!

Boots, Jet and I then proceeded to bounce our way over to where the girls had gone. The feeling of freedom in this jello land was awesome. We bounced and bounced and laughed and laughed. This was so much fun and everyone here in Jelloland couldn't stop laughing.

We bounced over to one of the jello houses and bounced our way inside. The kids inside were pushing each other into the walls and laughed hilariously as they bounced off, hit the ceiling, back to the floor and then back off the walls. It was such great fun!

All the kids were eating the jello too as they played, and even we had to try some of this awesome looking treat! I had never had jello and although the texture was very strange to me, it did taste very sweet. I noticed the other dogs were enjoying bites of it too!

"Well?" Maureen questioned with a big smile across her little face. "Did you expect anything like this?"

"I guess not!" I exclaimed, still bouncing on the jello floors.

"This is a riot!" Jacques yelled and jumped out the window and back on to the jello yard.

We all laughed at his crazy antics; he so enjoyed having fun! Maureen and I followed Jacques bouncing out the window and then down one of the orange jello streets. We jumped on to a jello rainbow and slid down into a little valley filled with jello flowers whose petals were every different color you could imagine.

This place was so colorful and pleasant to behold; I just felt all cheerful inside, if that makes any sense. I could look across Jelloland and see hundreds of children and even babies bouncing happily, laughing and singing and even dancing as they bounced along the way. Abby, Karen, and Kathy finally caught up with us. We must have bounced along for miles because we couldn't see the road that we had come in on.

I looked again across this lovely landscape and noticed a wide waterfall and river that looked brown. It seemed very out of place amid such color and as I pointed it out to the kids they began to run full speed toward these falls.

Jacques, who was always the fastest when there was something new to explore, ran a little too fast, and as he bounced clumsily on the jello he landed face first in the river. He turned quickly and to our surprise, as we caught up to him, looked up licking his chops dripping in rich creamy chocolate.

"Hey Jacques," Maureen laughed. "Now you're a chocolate lab!"

We all laughed hysterically and jumped into the chocolate river to join him. It was amazing. Children were floating under the chocolate waterfall with their mouths open catching the delectable treat as it dripped like honey from the jello rocks! The girls were screaming in glee, running all around getting soaked in the wonderful treat.

This was so far beyond my own imagination that all I could do was enjoy it. Here in heaven chocolate wasn't harmful to us dogs like it was on earth and we could eat to our hearts content. We played in the falls and the river until we were filled to the brim with chocolate. When we climbed out of the river we were completely clean and Jacques was once again his old yellow self!

"Wow, that was awesome," Jet remarked. "Who would have ever thought!"

"Hey you guys," Karen said with a look of mischief in her eyes, "let's go over to the ice cream shop," and she pointed down the jello road to a row of little shops.

"Sounds good to me," I excitedly replied, "Ice cream is my favorite!" Frankly, I didn't know how I could eat anything more after all that chocolate, but I loved ice cream!

We happily bounced our way over to the shops and went into the one that displayed, 'Ice Cream.' As we looked over the counter at the different flavors I noticed that each one had little chunks of jello frozen into the ice cream making it look very colorful and appetizing too!

"Imagine that," Karen squealed, "jello ice cream!"

We all laughed at the thought and proceeded to order our favorite flavors from a kindly woman whose eyes danced with pure joy! She was so sweet to all of us and made sure the girls got lots of sprinkles and cherries on their jello ice cream sundaes, and gave each of us dogs a jello bowl to eat our ice cream from that we could even eat after the ice cream was licked clean!

"There sure was nothing like this on earth!" Kathy exclaimed, "and if there were I'm sure my mother would never have let me eat all this sugar!"

We all laughed again at that comment knowing none of us would have ever eaten anything remotely close to this.

Many people were gathered around the shops and enjoying all they had to offer and we constantly heard laughter as they couldn't help but bounce on the jello sidewalks. It was funny to watch because walking was out of the question here....you had to bounce along the way!

"Well Maureen," I began to say, "You were right. We would have never dreamed about a place like this! God surely has surprised us this time for sure. Even the greatest imagination could never have thought up something as fun and as this."

"Or as colorful," Karen added. "It's just so pretty here, all these colors everywhere you look!"

It was truly very colorful. Everything was so bright and happy looking.

I looked around and noticed Jacques and Jet were standing a ways off talking to a group of young boys. They were very focused on what the boys were sharing and looked rather serious, considering where we were at the moment. I bounced over to where they were, the girls and Boots following close behind me, still eating their ice cream and laughing.

"What's up guys? I asked curiously.

"These boys were telling us about a huge park they just came from where dinosaurs live," Jacques replied anxiously with anticipation in his voice.

I knew instantly that this is where Jacques would want to go next, and I was right, when one of the boys, whose name was Brandon, asked if he'd like to see them. Without a moment's hesitation, Jacques was already bouncing ahead.

Looking back at us he yelled, "Hey what are you waiting for?" So the boys quickly jumped ahead of Jacques to lead the way to the next adventure.

The rest of us just looked at each other, let out a hearty laugh, and bounced our way behind the boys and Jacques. Jet, who had caught up to Jacques, was now walking by his side. So off we went to a new and different land.

Chapter Twenty-One

Nothing is Forgotten in Heaven

Next thing we knew we were on one of the roads of light once again and proceeded to drift over hills and forests until we could see a huge rocky plateau down below with vegetation that was larger than anything I had seen up until now. Giant trees, whose branches spread out like wings, covered the landscape and flowers and plants that must have been thirty or forty feet high and very wide spread out among the humongous rolling meadows for what seemed like miles. As usual music permeated the atmosphere and the fragrance of these giant flowers filled our senses with delight.

We continued floating on the road a little further and there they were down below looking like giant creatures from another world. Hundreds of dinosaurs were walking all around the park; some eating lazily from the trees and others trudging through one of the many lakes that dotted the land in the distance. They were truly a magnificent creation and their size alone caused all of us to just stare in awe and wonder of God's amazing imagination.

There were many other people walking around the park too and some were even riding on some of the dinosaurs who, of course, were very friendly and obliging. We could hear children laughing and see them playing silly games with some of the smaller dinosaur babies among the trees.

"Well this is an awesome place for sure!" Jacques blurted out jumping off the road of light. "Let's look around."

We all jumped off the moving road and began walking down the winding paths under the massive vegetation that filled the exotic landscape. I had never seen such huge flowers and plants anywhere else in heaven, but then again, there were no animals nearly as huge as these dinosaurs. We came upon a rocky ledge where we looked down over an impressively large valley filled with dinosaurs of every kind. I felt like an ant in comparison to these giant creatures.

"What ya looking at?" a deep voice spoke from behind the spot we were standing.

Without looking up Jet exclaimed, "We're looking at all those giant creatures down below!" and then proceeded to look up into the face of a giant Brontosaurus.

Jet must have jumped ten feet he was so startled by the size of the creature standing there and we all wondered how we hadn't heard him come up behind us.

"No need to be scared of me!" he exclaimed. "You don't have to worry; we're all friendly here just like everywhere in heaven," and he laughed a deep, but thoroughly pleasant laugh, engaging us to do the same.

"I was just startled by your size so close up," Jet explained and then moved closer to this gentle giant.

"My name is Willy," he said. "One of the little girls here named me after a character in a cartoon on earth and the name just stuck," he laughed.

"I'm Jet and these are my friends Boots, Jacques and Pal," Jet replied.

Brandon introduced himself and his friends and Maureen introduced the girls.

"Nice to meet a new group of friends," he cooed. "I love meeting all the new people and animals who visit this place, there's always so much to share."

"We just came from an awesome place called Jelloland," Maureen offered, "and these boys told us about this dinosaur park; so we all came to check it out. Everything is so big here!"

"Well that's because we're so big so everything needs to be the same," Willy laughed.

"Come with me, I'll take you on a tour and let you meet some of my friends here."

"Great!" Brandon exclaimed. "Dinosaurs are my favorite!"

"Feel free to hop on for a ride," Willy said inviting us to climb on to his long and very high back.

We all climbed up from his long tail and he began moving slowly toward the huge valley down below. All kinds of dinosaurs came up to meet us and introduced themselves like we had been long lost friends. It was an awesome place and everywhere we turned gigantic trees, flowers and plants of every color and shape graced the landscape. Huge prehistoric birds flew high over us and every once in a while landed nearby causing us to gasp at their incredible size. After a while, we grew used to the enormity of all this life that surrounded us and began to really enjoy the very different and diverse environment these creatures God first created lived in.

We finally arrived on the bottom of the plateau where we had first been standing. Looking up from this perspective was absolutely amazing. We all felt like miniature toys compared to everything that surrounded us. Several other people and their dogs came over to greet us and exclaimed with awe how impressed they were with this wondrous place.

"Have you ever imagined you'd actually see dinosaurs," one man said.

"This was only something I dreamed of," Brandon replied. "I was always so curious as to what they would really look like and now I know. Imagine this too; they're all so friendly. Not like they were on earth at all; at least not later in time when they became carnivorous."

"Yeah, not like we'd be standing here if they still were," Maureen laughed.

We walked all over the dinosaur park and explored the winding paths, huge caves and gardens that you could never imagine with a finite mind. This place was so incredible and so huge that it was almost incomprehensible. Yet here it stood; another incredible wonder in heaven.

We met all kinds of interesting people even a few who actually lived in mansions in this park. Some, who had been paleontologists, were absolutely thrilled with this marvelous environment. They were the ones who gave tours here and explained to those interested all the different species of plant and animal life. These people amazed me because they had such a passion for everything that lived here and really got excited when someone wanted to know more about these creatures of past times.

We thoroughly enjoyed the tour of the Dinosaur Park, especially with Willy as our guide, and Jacques suggested we return to our own park, go for another swim, which we all loved, and then get some more nourishment for our bodies; something that always brought such pleasure. So off we went catching the usual road of light, and headed back to our favorite meadow and lake.

As we arrived at our destination some of our best friends saw us and ran up to welcome us back, laughing and running in circles engaging us in a game of chase. Of course, we were obliging, and we ran straight for the lake making a humongous splash as we all flew into the water at once. Oh heaven! It's such a glorious and fun place and as I swam in the refreshing waters I couldn't help but think of JoAnne and the day we would be reunited forever in this wonderful home.

Chapter Twenty-Two

Celebrating God's Way

eaven is indeed a marvelous place and I couldn't begin to tell you all the rest of the adventures we dogs have had. Time doesn't exist here, as I have mentioned, and we never have to sleep as we never get tired. We just play, visit friends, and explore the glorious expanse of our heavenly home all the while waiting for the day when our loving masters will join us for eternity. By far the neatest thing here is the fact that we dogs have such expanded understanding compared to what we had on earth. We love that we can communicate by actually talking and know what everything means. I do need to share just one other experience we had though, as it was something we all had been waiting for. Let me explain.

One day, as the four of us were travelling on one of the roads of light, Marcus, the angel I had met when I first got here, suddenly showed up just ahead of us on the same road.

"Pal! Jet!" he called with excitement. "I have some great news for the two of you."

"What's up?" we simultaneously questioned.

"A member of your family is about to arrive here in heaven," he said, smiling and laughing at the same time. "It's time for you to see the Throne Room."

"Who is it?" I asked with anticipation.

"JoAnne's mother Frances," he answered, "Your other caregiver!"

"C'mon we can all go meet her at the gates."

This was indeed exciting as she was going to be the first of my immediate family to come home with us. And this would be an opportunity to see firsthand what happens to people when they first arrive here in heaven. I was particularly happy because she had been my caregiver after JoAnne had left for college and I had spent the last years of my life being close to her. Jet had never lived with her although, of course, he knew her because she was JoAnne's mom!

We all headed in the direction of heaven's huge gateway and as we got closer we could see many new arrivals climbing out of transports and being greeted by relatives and friends. The joy of these moments was indeed indescribable; joy like this exists in no other place and the singing and praise of the angels permeated the atmosphere.

Suddenly I saw her. She looked much younger than I remembered; but then again everyone here looked young. Even so, I knew without a doubt it was Frances. Her face glowed with joy and lit up even more when she was greeted by her own mother who had been here for many years by earth's time. She was ecstatic to see relatives and friends who had come here before her but never had I seen such joy as when Jesus Himself came up to greet her. Her face seemed to melt with love as He held out His hand to her then lovingly embraced her as He did everyone.

"Welcome home Frances," I heard Him say lovingly. "You are here to receive the rewards My Father will soon bestow upon you because you trusted in Me all your earthly life. We have prepared a place for you to abide with Us now for all eternity and never again will you know anything but joy and love."

He smiled warmly and Frances smiled back at Him as He took her hand. He then proceeded to lead her to the Throne Room. She walked next to Him, her white robe glimmering in the light of Jesus and we watched in awe as He led her up one of the four golden stairways to present her to His Father.

The Throne Room was definitely the most glorious place in heaven that I had ever seen. I was taken aback by all the activity and the variety of Creatures that surrounded the Throne of the Father and lived in this awesome and huge place. A brilliant rainbow surrounded the Throne of God and colors shot out in every direction. It was way beyond anyone's comprehension and the Living Creatures whose eyes, which were even in their wings, were looking everywhere. Nothing escaped their view.

Twenty four elder's sat on thrones worshipping and myriads of angels joined in the song of the Lamb. Holy Spirit, who looked like swirls of color was at the left side of the throne and there were thousands of people dancing, singing, and worshipping the God of all creation. A huge celebration was taking place welcoming all the new arrivals, including Frances. I realized at this moment that celebrating never ceases in the Throne room. It just continues all the time with people coming in and out wanting to spend time with the Father worshipping and loving Him.

As we watched Jesus hand her over to His Father, the Father took her hand, embraced her, and gently spoke.

"Frances my beloved child! Come celebrate your homecoming with all of heaven and reap the joy of believing in My Son Whom I sent for you! We have been waiting for you," and He proceeded to put a crown on her head and a beautiful robe glittering with jewels around her shoulders.

I had never seen Frances so happy and literally undone. All around the Throne angels and Seraphim, huge beings with fire coming out of their heads, flew about and worshipped and sang and praised the Father and everyone in the room danced and worshipped celebrating their loved ones homecoming.

Frances stood before the Father completely mesmerized. He held her for a while, speaking only to her, and even I could feel the waves of love that shot out everywhere from His being. The rainbow round about the Throne was spectacular! Waves of sapphire blue enveloped the stairs, then gorgeous deep purple, and then a teal color so amazing and large that it encompassed the top part of the throne. All the other colors followed; green, yellow, red, pink, all glowing brilliantly around the Father. These colors reflected off of everything including the white robes of God's people dancing about the room.

After the Father had welcomed her and spoken words of love and appreciation to her, Frances turned and was greeted by all her friends and relatives again who bid her to come and join in the party with them. Jesus Himself took her hand and began to dance like a groom would with His bride. It was all so amazing. I felt like I was floating on air just from partaking of the beauty and love of this place.

After her dance with Jesus I walked over to where Frances was celebrating and as soon as she saw me and she bent over and wrapped her arms around my neck.

"Pal, you sweet baby! I'm so glad to see you too!"

I wagged my tail heartily and whispered into her ear, "Welcome to heaven Frances, we've been waiting for you," and at that moment Jet peeked his head out from behind me wagging his tail exuberantly and chanted "Welcome, welcome, to our wonderful home!"

"Jet!" she exclaimed jubilantly. "You're here too!"

Frances laughed heartily and began dancing with her brother-in-law Al and her mother Mary. All her other relatives and friends happily greeted her and they all took turns dancing and worshipping together. They all looked so happy and Jesus Himself joined again in the celebration and danced with everyone. It was indeed a sight to behold and the worship overwhelmed all of us as we celebrated together.

I don't know how long we stayed in the Throne room by earth's standards but it was a long time. Celebration in heaven is far different than anything on earth. It's all encompassing and you literally feel the love rushing inside you, like it's actually part of your being. And here it is!

The party for all new arrivals is simply astounding. It seemed odd to me that back on earth death was so grim, when up here, the biggest party of your life is happening. That, I know, is one day about to change as God will show the earth what really does happen up here; but that's for another time!

It was now time for Frances to enjoy one of the greatest things humans experience in heaven. Seeing her mansion for the first time! Everyone was encouraging her to go to her to go there; the place God had prepared just for her. The Father makes sure each mansion is special, accentuating the gifts of each individual. Everyone is completely amazed the first time they see their new home. Her friends and relatives were anxious to let her see all the gifts they had been saving for her for this special time.

So everyone gathered together, including Jet and I, and joyously began down one of the roads of light towards her mansion. We all were singing and dancing, happy to engage in a new journey with someone we loved so much. We knew that Frances would now enjoy the wonder of living in our amazing heavenly home forever.

The End

If you would like to know more about what heaven is really like, I suggest you take the time to read Kat Kerr's books. Kat has been taken to heaven for 16 years and has revelation that will truly bless you.

To order your book today contact:
One Quest International @ 904-527-1943

CPSIA information can be obtained at www.ICGtesting.com
Printed in the USA
BVOW10s1652141113

336292BV00001B/1/P

9 781628 399974